ALSO BY MICHAEL FEDO:

The Lynchings in Duluth
One Shining Season
Chronicles of Aunt Hilma
The Man From Lake Wobegon
One Bad Dude (with Ted Jefferson)

Indians In the Arbor- vitae

a novel by

Michael Fedo

bgp

2002
New York
Green Bean Press

INDIANS IN THE ARBORVITAE. © 2002 by Michael Fedo.

All rights reserved. Printed in the United States of America. No part of this book may be used or reproduced in any manner whatsoever without written permission from the publisher except in the case of brief quotations embodied in critical articles and reviews. For information, address:

Green Bean Press
P.O. Box 237
New York, NY 10013 USA
718-965-2076 ph/fax
ian@greenbeanpress.com

ISBN 1-891408-30-5
Library of Congress Control Number: 2002116843

Cover image and author photo by Judith Fedo.
Design by Judith Fedo and Ian Griffin.

ACKNOWLEDGEMENTS

Portions of this book, in somewhat different form, originally appeared in *The North Dakota Quarterly, The North American Review, America West Airlines Magazine* and *The Fiction Quarterly.*

The author is indebted to the Anderson Center for Interdisciplinary Studies for awarding him two month-long residencies during which this story developed.

For a complete list of titles published by Green Bean Press, as well as information about upcoming projects, special deals, free downloads and other cool stuff, visit us online.
http://www.greenbeanpress.com

For Glenn,
who knows his arborvitae.

Chapter One

Before Richard Fundy left his fourth period American Studies classroom at Button Gwinnet Senior High School, he divided his students into five small groups for the purpose of discussing why loud farts don't stink. "Do whatever research you believe necessary, and come prepared for a dialogue on the subject tomorrow," he said. As pupils assembled, Richard excused himself and left the room.

In the office he filed an absence report with Dorothy, the principal's secretary, and turned toward the door.

"Oh, Mr. Fundy," Dorothy said, "are you—um—sure about the reason you've given for your absence?"

"Beg pardon?" Richard wiped perspiration from his temple with a handkerchief.

"Are you sure you want 'Heartsick—lack of succor' on this official form as your reason for missing class?"

"Yes, of course." Richard caught her studying him, arching a brow, peering over the top of her half-glasses.

"Well, all right then," she sighed. "Anyway, I hope you're soon feeling better, Mr. Fundy."

"Thank you, Dorothy. That's very kind."

As Richard pulled into the driveway of the clapboard house on Mister Lane that he shared with his widowed father Elwood in the village of Mechebois, near the paper mill town of Cloquet, he noticed Elwood's 1974 Checker idling near the mailbox. Elwood, a wiry, slightly stooped man of 69, was crouched behind the south wall of the detached garage, 12-gauge shotgun in hand. The old man squinted and stepped quickly into the driveway, firing both barrels in the direction of the arborvitae shrubs bordering the north edge of the property. The recoil propelled him two steps backward. "You cowardly sons of bitches," he hollered. "Stay the hell away from here." Elwood lowered the gun and stood trembling, spittle gathering at the corners of his mouth.

Richard leaped from his minivan. "Dad! What's going on?"

"Get down, Dickie! Get down!" Elwood shouted.

Richard crouched behind his car. "What's wrong, Dad?"

Elwood jammed two more shells into the breech. He raised the weapon and cautiously approached the row of arborvitae. He poked through the branches. "Damn, missed 'em again." Then he turned toward his son, who was now standing in the middle of the driveway, holding his head. "Indians," Elwood said, shaking his head. "From the Fond du Lac reservation. They like to hide behind these arborvitae. Soon as they know you're gone they raid the house."

"Dad," Richard said with a nervous chortle, "that's nuts. Indians don't hide in hedges. There's nobody there. Good grief, you can't go around shooting a weapon like that. You could hurt someone."

"I should damn well hope so." Elwood cleared his throat and spat. "They like to take advantage of the elderly, Dickie." He emptied the shells from his shotgun, and approached his son.

"Dad," Richard said softly, "let me have that thing." He reached for the 12-gauge as Elwood drew back.

"Oh, no. This doesn't leave me, Dickie. Not these days."

"Okay, Dad," Richard said, palms up. "Tell me what brought this on."

"All those years of gallivanting made you forget how things are in the country, Dickie." Elwood sat on a fat oak stump and lit a cigarette. He said about 10 years ago Richard's late mother wanted an arborvitae border along the driveway. She thought it would be more attractive than a snow fence, and would serve the same purpose of keeping wind-driven snow from filling in the driveway. "I told her, 'Rae, that's exactly what the Indians are looking for. When those hedges get high enough they'll hide out back there and spy on the house.'" He exhaled through his nostrils. He looked at the cigarette and flicked ashes before speaking again. "You know they got them cell phones. So when nobody's home, they right away call their buddies who got trucks, and then come in and strip the house. There's businessmen right here in town—I could name names—who encourage them. They got markets down in Chicago where they sell the stuff so cops around here can't trace it. Happens all the time." He coughed up phlegm and spat again. "Damned arborvitae. We got to get rid of it."

Richard Fundy was a 43 year-old first-year teacher. He had worked 17 years as a claims adjuster at Blessed Assurance Life and Casualty but had quit three years earlier when redundancy set in, close on the heels of his divorce. Following these reversals, he returned to his alma mater, Babiole College, to pick up a teaching certificate. He was immediately hired at Button Gwinnet, because according to Hulot Piquete, the principal, he was the only applicant able to identify the school's namesake as a signer of the Declaration of Independence.

Since the school was in Brackett, just nine miles from his father's home, it seemed natural for him to move back and occupy his old boyhood bedroom.

In the month since he'd returned, evenings were spent watching television, with silences occasionally broken by Elwood requesting Richard fetch him a beer or Dr. Pepper from the refrigerator. "I could get it myself, Dickie," his father would say, "but think of it as your rent. You can't beat that for cheap."

This afternoon, Elwood abandoned the Jerry Springer show just as two participants started wrestling after haranguing over whether "animus" and "animist" meant the same thing. Elwood stared out the window at the arborvitae. "I think I see movement out there, Dickie," he said. "Sun's reflectin' off their binoculars."

Richard went out to the shrubs to assuage his father, walking behind them, pushing through, and making a great show that there was no one in the arborvitae.

"They're quick, Dickie," Elwood said. "They ain't gonna sit there and wait for you. They got their escape routes all planned out. You gotta catch 'em at their own game. Sneak up and give 'em a swift kick in the gazoons."

That evening, while eating macaroni and cheese dinners and watching Peter Jennings deliver the news, Elwood asked Richard to dig up the bushes.

Richard sucked a bit of noodle from a bicuspid. "Well, all right. If it'll give you peace of mind, I'll take care of them after school tomorrow."

"The both of us'll rest a whole lot easier when we can survey the territory all around us," Elwood said. "The Indians and their pals won't be sneakin' up on the house and rippin' us off."

Richard sighed. "I'm heartsick, Dad."

"I know whatcha mean," his father returned. "So you wanna watch a movie later? Maybe they got something with Clint Eastwood. Ever since old John Wayne died, I don't like movies much. But I don't mind Clint Eastwood." Elwood blew his nose into a blue bandana with white polka dots. He folded it and looked at his son.

"I left school today because I was heartsick," Richard said.

"Yeah, I heard you," Elwood said. He scratched the stubble on his chin.

It occurred to Richard that he'd never seen his father shave. Yet the beard was never longer than stubble. He couldn't recall if his father had even shaved for Rae's funeral. That three-day shadow used to drive his mother crazy. "Go in and shave, El," she'd say. "Do it for me."

After classes the following day, Hulot Piquete was sitting at his desk, his back to the door, when Richard Fundy knocked. "Fundy—been expecting you," the principal said, not facing Richard. A manila folder with RICHARD FUNDY typed on the tab was on the desk, and Dr. Piquete held several sheets of paper in his fleshy, pink hands. He was a robust, tidy man with a thin gray mustache. Tiny spectacles rested on the end of his nose.

Swiveling around, frowning, Dr. Piquete confronted Richard. "I've got lots of questions today, Fundy. First, though, I'm not quite sure what to make of this report. This is a new one."

"Sir?" Richard looked at the vacant chair in the principal's office, but was not invited to sit. He rested his hand on it, then noticed Dr. Piquete wasn't wearing his shoes, which were beneath the desk.

"It doesn't strike you the least bit odd—your reason for yesterday's absence?" Dr. Piquete picked a bit of fluff from the lapel of his gray suit. "Heartsick? From lack of succor?" He looked expectantly at Richard who nodded.

"Yes," Richard said.

"Yes? Only yes?" Dr. Piquete paused. "I don't want to be hard-nosed about this, Fundy. I know teachers get sick—flu, colds, plantar warts—which I myself endure on the balls of both feet. Painful devils. Then there's broken ankles, carpal and tarsal tunnel syndromes, bipolar depressions, migraine headaches, impacted wisdom teeth, diarrhea, pulmonary edema, scleroderma, sciatica, seborrheic keratoses, squamous-cell skin cancer, chronic bronchitis, pleurisy, psittacosis...." He looked at Richard again, and waved his hand. "I could go on. In my 22 years at the helm of Button Gwinnet, I've encountered all manner of ills that flesh is heir to."

"You've witnessed a number of ailments," Richard offered, and sat.

"Oh, sorry, Fundy. Go ahead and sit down. Sit down. We might be here a while."

"In that case, would it be all right if I phoned my father? He's worried about the Indians, and I haven't had time yet to dig out the arborvitae. He's expecting me to do that first thing this afternoon."

"This shouldn't take that long, Fundy," Dr. Piquete said, narrowing his eyes. "Problems with Indians and arborvitae?"

"Sort of." Richard shrugged. "But I'd rather not go into that now."

Dr. Piquete scratched the bottom of one foot with the other, grimacing as he did. "I'm concerned about your perceived lack of succor."

"Me too," Richard said.

Dr. Piquete looked at Richard. After an awkward silence, the principal spoke. "It may not have occurred to you, but I take this quite personally. Of all my achievements as principal at Button Gwinnet, I've been known as a teacher's administrator. I stand behind my people. I support them. It's been the hallmark of my career. And then to receive a report from a new staff member making what I feel is a specious claim, well, frankly, Fundy, it hurts." Dr. Piquete tapped his heart with his fist.

Richard nodded.

The principal held up a pink copy of the absence report. "Anyway, this form goes directly to the board office. Did you know that?"

"I never gave it a thought. I simply stated why I had to leave school." Richard glanced at the slightly askew print of Washington crossing the Delaware above Dr. Piquete's desk.

Dr. Piquete cleared his throat. "Let me put it to you this way, Fundy," he said, fingering his pocket organizer. "If you were in my shoes right now, would you sign this report and pass it along to the superintendent's office?"

"Not to put too fine a point on it, Dr. Piquete, but even you aren't in your shoes right now," Richard said, staring at the principal's stocking feet.

Dr. Piquete frowned. "Very droll, Fundy," he said, reaching for another sheet of paper. "What I'm going to do with your absence report is pass it along with a disclaimer. I'm not at all sure 'heartsick' will fly downtown, but *I* may have to answer for this so-called lack of succor. A conscientious principal always endeavors to provide an environment conducive to the comfort of his teachers. You see, it all comes back to me, and I'm at a loss here. So maybe you can help me understand. You have to know these things are taken very seriously by the administration. Every now and then we get some wise guy in the system who figures nobody reads these reports. A few years back, we had this young fellow in math who was from your old college, Babiole. Anyway, he thought he'd be real smart, and one time wrote his reason for absence in Latin. Figured he'd put one over on us. Well, it happens Dr. Kerry at the board office had a second major in romance languages. She reads it, and everything hits the fan. See, Fundy, this fellow wrote he was absent because he thought he was turning into a cat. We don't tolerate frivolous shenanigans, Fundy. It erodes discipline.

"As you can well imagine, his days were quickly numbered in this district. I trust you catch my drift." The principal spun around and extracted more forms from Richard's file. "It has come to my attention that you've routinely taken your classes on disparate tangents. Like yesterday, for instance." He stared at Richard. "Your fourth hour class before you got—heartsick. It's one thing to have fun in class, but flatulence? There's core material to be covered here. And let me tell you, we've had several calls from parents about your topic. Flatulence is not an American study, Fundy. Flatulence is not merely an American phenomenon, as it knows no international boundary or creed. You need to stick to the basics of *American* studies, which you've been hired to teach. On a personal note, I often held the emissions from the paper mills carried the odor of a great wind-breaking, but I don't go around treating it in a jocular manner with pupils. A sense of decorum must always be maintained."

Richard sighed. "The kids have had trouble focusing, so I thought maybe that topic would generate some enthusiasm."

Shaking his head, the principal said, "Do I understand you just skimmed the unit on 19th century American industrialists in favor of your attempt to amuse those pupils? Well, they weren't amused, Fundy."

Dr. Piquete exhaled audibly. "Crepitation, if you will, is not listed on any form as part of the graduation standards for this district." He grimaced briefly. "And never will be. But the captains of industry are."

"The way that unit is structured in the text is boring in my opinion," Richard said. He felt a trickle of moisture in his armpits.

"They may well be boring, but it's a district requirement, and individual teachers do not have the option of avoiding those portions of the curriculum they don't like." Dr. Piquete rifled through more papers, culling one from the stack on his desk. "For a man of your age and experience I'd have expected more."

Richard glanced at his watch, then lowered his eyes.

Dr. Piquete grunted. "I know you want to look after your father, Fundy, so I'll try to make this quick. I'm going to give you a second chance. I will put this behind us and forge ahead with the expectation that you will endeavor to modify your act, so to speak.

I'll turn in your absence report, and take the heat on it if necessary. For this you owe me, Fundy." He paused. "Here's your part of the bargain. Not so much for me, actually, but for our entire scholastic community."

Richard crossed his legs, loosened his tie.

Dr. Piquete clapped Richard on the knee. "I've conducted informal surveys in the hallways off and on during the last several years. And sadly, no one associated with Button Gwinnet Senior High School, save the two of us, has the foggiest notion who Button Gwinnet was. I'm going to schedule an all-school assembly, invite parents and folks from the community, and have this man's name and role in American history clarified. I'd like you to do the lecture, Fundy. You won't let us down, now will you?"

Richard swallowed. Recalling an undergraduate paper he'd written on the signers of the Declaration, Button Gwinnet was primarily known for his unique name.

"Well, Fundy, are you up to the task?" Dr. Piquete persisted.

"Sure," Richard said, pondering how to put the best spin on the brief life and minimal accomplishments of Button Gwinnet. "Why not?"

Back at home, Richard changed into jeans and a sweatshirt. He grabbed a spade from the garage and went to the arborvitae. As he drove it into the soil, he detected motion behind the shrubbery. Hoisting the shovel to his shoulder, he cautiously stepped toward the hedgerow. A dark-haired man about Richard's age was on his hands and knees. "Hey, what's going on here?" Richard called.

"Tossed a ball for my dog," the man said. "Little guy couldn't find it, so I thought I'd help him out. But I don't see it either." The man looked up at Richard and nodded. "Don't I know you?" he said. "You're Rich Fundy, aren't you? Remember me—Luther Durfee? Actually, I now go by Luther Burgess-Durfee. You live here?"

"Yeah," Richard said. He recalled Luther Durfee from Cloquet High School, where 25 years ago Luther had been valedictorian, won a Merit scholarship, and matriculated to Eastman in Rochester, where he became a percussionist in a symphony orchestra. "What're you doing around here? Vacation?"

"Sort of. I'm on sabbatical." Luther grinned. "I've been the associate conductor of the Duluth Symphony down in Georgia."

Richard regarded Burgess-Durfee. He was wearing faded jeans, a faded blue long-sleeved T-shirt and $150 Nikes. "Where's your dog?"

"Oh, he's around. You know how dogs are. Probably taking a whizz in somebody's yard."

"You been by before?" Richard asked, lowering the spade.

"Probably. Come by a couple times a week when I walk Johann. That's his name, Johann Strauss the Younger. Why do you ask?"

"Well, it's my dad," Richard said, nodding toward the house. "He's got this notion that Indians are hiding behind these arborvitae spying on the house, just waiting for him to vacate so they can rip him off."

Luther nodded. "Well, tell him it isn't this Indian. In fact, this is my first time near those shrubs."

"I was a claims adjuster for 17 years," Richard said. "Got laid off, went back to college to get a teaching certificate. I'm at Brackett High—which the principal insists we call Button Gwinnet—teaching American Studies this year."

"No kidding. I'm supposed to be composing music on my sabbatical," Luther said. "Our orchestra down in Duluth commissioned me to write a polka suite for accordions and mandolins. Then a *scherzo* for dobro and didjeridoo." He scuffed the ground with his shoe. "The symphony orchestra world is changing, my friend. Expanding horizons, you might say, blending various forms, crossing over. Our new manager is a real go-getter. They're trying to schedule a concert staging of *Fidelio*, and get this, they want to have Garth Brooks and Reba McEntire do it."

"I'd probably see it," Richard said. "Might pull me out of this malaise, you know, with Dad and all." Richard stuck the spade in the ground. "The cockles of my heart have grown cold, Luther." He looked at Luther, then back at the house. "Hey, you want to come in for a beer? Maybe I could get one of your Ojibwe remedies for my condition."

"Beer sounds fine, but I don't know one Native American cure for anything. I hardly knew I was Ojibwe. Remember my dad was a Unitarian minister. He didn't talk much about the old ways. We always take ibuprofen at our house."

"I think that's for headaches, Luther," Richard said as the two ambled toward the house.

Inside, Richard walked to the television set and snapped it off. Elwood looked up. "We got company, Dad," he said, indicating Luther Burgess-Durfee. "This is an old classmate from high school, Luther Durfee. But now he's Luther Burgess-Durfee. Luther, this is my dad, Elwood."

Elwood rose, warily regarding Luther before extending his hand. As he turned toward the kitchen, Elwood whispered, "Right in the gazoons, Dickie." He pantomimed an elbow shot, before going through the doorway.

Richard followed. "Luther's a symphony conductor and a composer, Dad. Jeez, he was our valedictorian in high school. His father was a preacher."

"Where'd you find this guy, Dickie?"

"You'll never believe this, Dad." Richard chuckled. "He was in the arborvitae."

"It's in their blood, Dickie," Elwood said, scowling. "And now he's inside, he'll case the joint. They'd love to get their hands on a lot of this stuff."

"Look, I'm going to grab a couple beers. You come on and join us if you want."

"I suppose I better," Elwood said. "Somebody's got to look out for my property."

"Dad," Richard started, opening the refrigerator. "Be careful now. Luther is a well-educated, professional person who's not in the least bit interested in stealing anything from this house. He's not a crook, Dad." Richard grabbed three bottles of beer and carried them to the living room.

Luther was sitting in Elwood's recliner with his feet propped. "Neat chair," he said. "I've been thinking of getting one of these myself."

"I bet you have," said Elwood, eyeing Richard.

"Dad," Richard said softly, forcing a smile. He handed a beer to Luther, who quickly twisted off the cap and took a long swallow.

"I've been divorced a couple years," Richard said, sitting on the sofa. "No kids. How about you?"

Luther covered a burp with his hand. "Got two boys, 14 and 7. They're with their mother, going to school in Duluth. And Jezebel is teaching at a community college, publishing poems with literary presses. She has a nice career." He grinned. "Funny that a preacher's kid would marry a woman named Jezebel, don't you think?"

Elwood was sitting on a settee opposite Luther, cradling his beer bottle in his lap and frowning. "Seems more funny that you'd have one of those hyphenated last names," he said.

Richard groaned, but Luther smiled. "How so?" he asked.

"Like I've said a hundred times to Dickie, our society is doomed. Now it may not look like much to you, Mr. Burgess-Duffy, but—"

"Durfee, Dad," Richard interjected. "His name is Burgess-Durfee."

"Never mind," said Luther after taking another long swallow of beer. "I'd like to hear what this doomsday philosopher has to say."

"Don't laugh," Elwood said. "I never went to college like you fellas, but I know a few things." He tapped his nose. "Now you take this hyphenating of names. Don't seem like a big thing, and lots of folks are doing it. But it helps destroy what used to be a pretty good society."

"This I gotta hear," Luther said, leaning forward.

Richard moaned. "Dad, I think—"

"No, I want to hear what he thinks, Rich."

"Okay, we'll use you as an example, Luther Burgess-Durfee." Elwood stood, placing his beer on the mantel. "You got two boys. One of 'em grows up and wants to marry a girl who's also hyphenated. Let's say she's a Staufer-Haig. So now you got Mr. and Mrs. Staufer-Haig-Burgess-Durfee. They have a kid who grows up and marries a Henderson-Jenkins-McKinley-O'Hara. So now whadda we got? A family called Staufer-Haig-Burgess-Durfee-Henderson-Jenkins-McKinley-O'Hara. And of course, you got first names and maybe middle names on top of that. You boys see where I'm headed? Before too long, we'll have a family with enough names to take up a whole phone book by themselves.

"Now it don't take a genius to figure things out. If you need practically an entire telephone book to list the name of one or two families, we'll have to cut down more forests to make paper. That drives the cost of it to the moon. Besides that, pretty damn quick, there's practically no more trees on the planet, and everybody's dyin' pell-mell, because there ain't no oxygen for them to breathe. And why is that, boys? It's because so-called modern thinking folks are hyphenating their names. Laugh if you want, but I figure we're staring eyeball to eyeball with the end of modern civilization."

After a brief interlude while Elwood retrieved his beer, Richard said, "See, Luther? This is how it is."

"You can't deny the perverse logic in his argument, Rich."

"Logic?" Richard's brow furrowed. "I don't see—"

"So you're a musician," Elwood interrupted loudly, nodding at Luther. "Can you tune a piano? We ain't touched ours since Dickie's mama died eight years ago."

Luther strode to the spinet beneath a print of Christ in Gethsemane. He ran several scales and winced. "She's got some sour spots. But sure, I could come over and tune it for you one of these days."

"Hey, that'd be all right," Elwood said. He approached his son and leaned in, cupping a hand to Richard's ear.

"I know, Dad," Richard started. "I can forget about the old gazoons for now."

"Right, Dickie." Elwood smiled. "Another beer, Luther?" Without waiting for a reply, Elwood moved to the kitchen, calling as he opened the refrigerator. "How'd you take to music so good, Luther? Me and his mother tried like hell to get Dickie to learn the piano. But he was stubborn as a mule, and couldn't play nothin' very well. Remember, Dickie?"

Elwood returned with a beer for Luther. "Did you want another, too, Dickie? There's more in the fridge." He jerked his head toward the kitchen.

Luther accepted the beer and nodded. "It wasn't widely known, but my father had played in jazz and swing bands in a previous incarnation. He was a drummer, and if I wouldn't practice he'd take my sticks and rap paradiddles and rim shots on my noggin. When the choice boils down to paradiddles on your head or practice a half hour, you don't have to think twice."

"I used to rap Dickie's knuckles but it didn't do no good," Elwood said. "Never knocked on his noggin though." He sighed. "Probably should have." He rested his hand on Luther's shoulder. "I don't suppose Dickie's told you about your tribesmen from Fond du Lac hiding back of my arborvitae."

"Yes, he has, Mr. Fundy." Luther looked up at Elwood.

Richard, moaning, shaded his eyes with his hand.

"Maybe you could talk to them," Elwood said. "Every once in a while I fire my 12-gauge more or less to scare 'em off. But I hate to think of doing that for the rest of my life. And Dickie can't shoot any better than he plays the piano."

"Geez, Dad." Richard began, his face flushed. "Luther, I'm sorry. There are no Indians, there's nobody out there, I mean..."

Luther chuckled. "Have Rich remove those hedges and your troubles are over."

"I like this guy, Dickie," Elwood said. "He went right to the heart of the issue. He seen what needs to be done. You was sort of namby-pamby. And you didn't take care of them arborvitae this afternoon. You come in here and drunk up my beer instead."

"Oh, Dad," Richard said, his shoulders sagging.

"Don't be harsh with him, Mr. Fundy," Luther said. "He's a good guy. Maybe he just listens to a different drummer."

"You're the drummer, Luther, not Dickie. Remember, Dickie quit on the piano. But I don't suppose he'da made much of a drummer either."

After dinner Richard carried a satchel of old college papers and texts from the garage into the kitchen and arranged them on the table. From yellowed manila folders he extracted his research files on the original signers of the Declaration of Independence. He frowned, spying the notes he'd recorded 22 years earlier on Button Gwinnet. By all accounts a failure in life and politics, the old Button was renowned only for his curious name, and because fate enabled him to join the more famous signers of the Declaration. To name a school after him must have been some wag's joke on a history-challenged community.

Gwinnet's public service was brief—a term as justice of the peace, two years in the Continental Congress, and a two-month appointment as acting governor of Georgia. His desire for a commission as a colonel in the army was denied, and in May, 1777, he was shot in a duel, dying several days later from a gangrenous infection. His burial site remains uncertain.

Anguished about what he'd say to Hulot Piquete the next day, Richard went to bed thinking he might need to invent a noble legend for Button Gwinnet to not disappoint the principal. But the notion plagued him, and he dozed fitfully before being roused.

"Dickie, wake up," Elwood was saying, poking his son. "I can't sleep."

Richard rolled toward Elwood, shielding his eyes from the light in the hallway outside his room. "Dad—geez. What time is it?"

"I dunno. One-thirty, two. But I can't rest. I wonder if you'd go downstairs and see if you can find that tape, 'Banjos at Bedtime' in the desk next to the TV stand. Might help me relax."

Richard slowly drew himself to a sitting position. Rubbing his eyes, squinting at his father, he cleared his throat. "Was it really necessary to wake me for this, Dad? I mean, it isn't exactly an emergency." Richard stood.

Elwood's visage softened. "It ain't easy gettin' old, Dickie. I don't have that much energy, you know? I read once where a person is allotted just so many heartbeats and then bango—that's all she wrote. Between you and me, Dickie, I don't think I have that many heartbeats left. I figure with you here and all, I could maybe save a few of them and prolong what's left of my appointed days. They say most heart attacks occur after a restless night in bed."

"Okay, Dad," Richard said with a resigned sigh. He started down the stairs, calling back as he descended. "You want anything else? A little warm milk, maybe?"

"No milk, Dickie. Gives me terrible indigestion." There was a pause while Elwood flicked his lighter and fired a cigarette. "I hate to be a bother, son, but would you mind going out and lookin' behind the arborvitae? I swear to God some Indian's out there." The stairs creaked as Elwood came down a step. "You gotta promise you'll dig 'em out tomorrow for sure." He heard his son rummaging through the desk. "Dickie, you hear me?"

CHAPTER TWO

On Tuesday morning as Richard stopped by the office to empty his mailbox, he could see Hulot Piquete's open door, the principal on the phone. Talking and gesticulating, Dr. Piquete beckoned Richard to enter as he concluded a conversation. Beaming, he looked at Richard. "I've been on the horn with Scheffel McPeece, president of The Carlton County Sanguine Society. We discussed your scholarship on Button Gwinnet, and guess what? They want you to address them on that subject. Sanguine Society folks are great people, Fundy," he said. "You should consider joining, though because of your schedule here, you'd have difficulty making their noon luncheons. Still, you'd be supporting them in spirit." He touched a pencil to the corner of his mouth. "There are maybe 15 of the faculty family at Button Gwinnet in the society, even though they can't attend the luncheons either. Of course, we'd find a substitute for your classes on the day you're scheduled so you could deliver the speech." Richard merely nodded, and the principal continued. "Think about it anyway, Fundy. Solid group. Wonderful chaps. Last year they purchased brand new football helmets for our varsity."

"Are they anything like the Odd Fellows?" Richard said.

Dr. Piquete allowed a fleeting smile. Waving his hand, he said, "Don't be silly, Fundy," then hollered to Dorothy to answer his ringing phone, take a message, and say he'd get back to the caller in ten minutes.

Returning to Richard, Dr. Piquete said, "Yes, yes, I know class will start momentarily. But here, I'll walk with you." Slipping into his shoes beneath his desk, he stood and ushered Richard from the office into the hallway. "I hailed you because I needed to ask you to be the main speaker," he said, smiling broadly.

"That's very kind of you, Dr. Piquete, but..."

"There's no problem, is there? Give you a chance to become acquainted with the chaps, who are really quite intrigued with your scholarship about Gwinnet. And of course, as you make your way among the members, you might wish to consider joining our number." Dr. Piquete touched Richard's shoulder. "I'll tell you frankly, Fundy, I think the world of these men. They're always completely supportive." He looked intently at Richard. "I emphasize this because these are gentlemen who spring to action when presented with problems. Or certain delicate issues in the life of a member."

"Thank you," Richard said, feeling himself flush. "However, I think I should tell you that Gwinnet—"

Richard was interrupted by hollering down the hall outside his classroom, and through the window he saw students throwing wads of paper at each other. As he was about to step into the room, Dr. Piquete barged past. The horseplay ceased, and the principal smiled benignly. He wagged his index finger at the pupils. "You folks know enough to busy yourselves in productive work while I have a word with Mr. Fundy outside," he said, as he turned toward the door.

"Dr. Piquete, I think—"

"Nonsense, Fundy. Bear down, boy. Bear down. You're no doubt concerned about how you were feeling the other day, and perhaps even anticipate a chronic condition. Get over it. You get over it by engaging yourself in meaningful work. Get outside yourself, as Nurse Narr likes to say. You met Hilda yet?"

Richard shook his head. He hadn't actually met Hilda Narr. But he had often noticed the blocky, craggy-faced woman with hennaed hair, leave her car in the faculty parking lot before school and walk quickly toward the building, waiting until she approached the door before snorting the last drag from a cigarette through her pursed lips.

"Golly, Hilda even predates me at Button Gwinnet. I don't suppose you knew that either," Dr. Piquete said as he wiped his glasses on his handkerchief before returning them to his face.

Richard peered into his classroom where chaos resumed. A textbook sailed toward the door, and as Richard opened it to keep it from smashing the window, Dr. Piquete stepped into the entry as the book flew by, knocking off his glasses.

"Enough already," Richard said, as the red-faced principal pushed him aside. "Now students," began Piquete, "the honorable thing to do here would be for the guilty party to own up to the deed. I'll ask this once: who threw the book?"

The room fell silent. Students' faces, framed in innocence, looked from Dr. Piquete to Richard Fundy, who cleared his throat and sat on his desk. "This won't do, people," he said. "At least one of you has allowed baser instincts to take over."

"We were bored, Mr. Fundy," one student hollered. "We missed you."

"We were heartsick," suggested another, and the room dissolved in laughter.

Richard turned toward Dr. Piquete, standing in the doorway, examining his bent glasses frames. "Who told them?" he whispered as the two stepped back into the hall.

"I could have been seriously injured here," the principal said.

"Yes, but I don't think it was wise to let them in—Oh, Lord," Richard moaned, and leaned against a bank of lockers.

Dr. Piquete held up his hand. "One thing at a time, please," he said through pinched lips. He held the wire frames in his hands, bending them to approximate their original shape. "This will have to do for now," he muttered, then straightened up and looked at Richard. "We'll get to the bottom of this, Fundy." Dr. Piquete placed the frames on his face. This look okay to you? Feel a bit awkward, but it'll have to do. Now, get in there and find the culprit or culprits." He fingered his glasses. "I don't like this one bit, Fundy."

"I understand." Richard sighed.

"Good." The principal started down the hall, then turned around. "One more thing. Please come to my office right after school today." With a wave of his hand Dr. Piquete pivoted smartly and headed down the hall, his leather heels tapping a staccato against the polished terrazzo.

Richard entered his room and offered $10 to anyone who would volunteer to be scapegoat regarding the book toss. A dozen hands shot up, and Richard opened his wallet, extracting three ten-dollar bills. Placing them on the table near the door, he said, "Work this out among yourselves," while slumping at his desk.

After dismissing his last class, Richard headed for the principal's office, but was intercepted by Hilda Narr. "Hello, Mr. Fundy," she called, in a gravelly, tobacco-ravaged voice. "We haven't been formally introduced, but I've had my eye on you since the first day of school this fall." She extended her hand, firmly grabbed his and shook it. "I'm Hilda," she said.

"Nice to meet you—Hilda." He turned toward the office. "I'm supposed to meet Dr. Piquete in a couple minutes."

"Yes, yes. He's told me all about you, Mr. Fundy. He said you were a man who'd bear watching, and I told him I'd already watched you. Poor fellow seems quite bereft, I told him." She smiled. "He was pleased I'd noticed, and suggested we have a little chat some time soon. You know you needn't suffer, Mr.—ah—Richard. Not at all. Sometimes just talking about things lifts the burden. It needn't be anything more than chatting over coffee some morning during your free period."

"Perhaps," Richard said, heading into the office. "Perhaps later."

"Ball's in your court, Richard Fundy," Hilda said, shrugging and lumbering down the hall.

Dr. Piquete stood in the office doorway, his face fixed in a warm smile. "I see you've finally met our Miss Narr," he said, beckoning Richard into his office, and indicating a chair for the teacher.

"I really hoped to bring you and Hilda together tonight, but she has some sort of family issue herself. Not all that unlike your own. Her father apparently believes himself a priest. Doesn't acknowledge fathering Hilda and her sister, Dorine. Claims to have taken vows of celibacy 60 years ago. So that plagues poor Hilda. Still, she's concerned about you, and is willing to do whatever it takes to bring you around." His smile faded to a frown as he sat behind his desk.

"Fundy, what do you know about the revisionists?" He slapped a sheaf of papers on the desk.

"Only that there are some scholars and historians who, upon further examination of the lives and actions of our foreparents, have determined that certain of our heroes were less than heroic. The controversy comes after they publish their findings or their speculations, I'm not sure which."

"They're everywhere," said Dr. Piquete. "As you know, I thought of spicing up your little Button speech and sort of filling in around the edges, as it were, with material and anecdotes about other prominent figures from the Revolutionary War period. Spent most of the day noodling over it, in fact. Had Dorothy download some stuff off the Internet, and was astonished at what neo-historians are attempting.

"These jokers are actually rewriting our history with the intention of finding skeletons in every closet. They load their computers with scandalous data about some national icon, while claiming another heroic figure was a pederast. Seems our esteemed primogenitors had more warts and blemishes than you could shake sticks at. They were scofflaws, womanizers; they performed unspeakable acts with domestic animals." Dr. Piquete was shaking his head. "There's not much on Gwinnet, but the whole notion of changing perceptions about our forefathers does give one pause."

"Pause, Dr. Piquete?"

"Yes. What I fear is that by exposing audiences to Gwinnet, the revisionists will discover him and throw him lock, stock and barrel in with those others they intend to trash. He deserves better. And it occurs to me the only way out of this is to fight fire with fire. We'll be better prepared than they, Fundy. I'm requesting you to continue your own diligent research on the matter. There's no offense stronger than truth. And truth needs no defense. But leave no doubt about it—we're going into the lions' den with this." The principal smiled, clapping Richard's shoulder. "But like the Biblical story of Daniel, no harm will befall us. Because we have the truth on our side. I'll bet Gwinnet was no saint, but those venerated pioneers in local education would not have named this institution after him had he not been a worthy individual."

"They must have had reasons," Richard said.

"So then," said Dr. Piquete, rising, indicating the doorway to Richard, "we'll talk more on this subject later." He quickly rose and dashed from the office as Richard was about to tell him the truth about Button Gwinnet.

At the Fundy residence on Mister Lane, as Elwood was walking from the mailbox back to the house, he heard rustling behind the arborvitae. He crept into the house, grabbed the 12-gauge, and in a hoarse whisper told Richard the Indians were back.

Not swayed this time, Richard glanced over the top of a travel brochure, *Guide to Orvieto, and Surrounding Umbrian Villages.* "Whatever, Dad," he said. "Just be careful with that thing."

Elwood lowered the weapon. "You mean you ain't coming with me, Dickie?"

"If I thought there was a problem, I'd be right there," Richard said. "But there's nobody in those arborvitae, Dad. Maybe you heard wind in the branches or something. If you have to take a look, go ahead. But I'm not getting all riled up over nothing."

"Damned arborvitae," Elwood growled. "If you'da dug them things up like you promised there'd be no place for Indians to lurk. But did you? You did not. Instead you sit there reading."

Richard sighed and folded the brochure. He'd been to Umbria once, to Orvieto with Claudia just before their divorce. They'd managed to avoid the Duomo prominently pictured on the cover of the travel brochure he now held in his hands. He'd sampled the Classico—the famous white wine of the region. Italians did not make a great white wine. If you wanted a good white, you drank German or French. Even Napa Valley. He'd not gone inside the Duomo at Orvieto, which upon his stateside return, everyone said was the whole purpose of riding the funicular up to the piazza.

Claudia had called him a turd for not going inside the Duomo. But she hadn't entered either. Claudia constantly carped about the absence of spaghetti and meatballs on menus. "I mean, haven't these people heard about Ragu or Paul Newman's spaghetti sauce for heaven's sake?"

In an Orvieto cafeteria they'd ordered a potently flavored squid antipasto, and tasted several mediocre wines. Two months after their return home, Claudia left.

Elwood's voice jolted Richard. "You could find me out there scalped, half-bleeding to death in the driveway, before it would mean anything to you. 'Course, it's only your crazy old man, and he don't count for squat." Elwood peeked through the front curtains, moved cautiously toward the door, opened it and stepped out. The door remained ajar.

He stood in the driveway and raised the gun as Luther Burgess-Durfee stepped through the shrubbery.

Luther's smile was strained "I'm sorry, Mr. Fundy," he said, approaching Elwood. "I didn't' mean to frighten you. But I was looking for my extra set of keys. I was hoping I'd dropped them here the other day while I was looking for Johann's ball." He chuckled. "I know what you think about Indians hanging out back there, but what can I say? You mind if I take another look?"

Elwood nodded warily and lowered the 12-gauge. "Geez, Luther, I coulda pulled the damn trigger. Hells bells, I don't want you out there unless I know it's you first. Otherwise, they might be lookin' for a new associate conductor down in Duluth. Know what I mean?"

Luther resumed his search amongst the shrubbery. "Yeah, I know. I should have called. But I didn't want to bother you. You might have been watching television."

Elwood shook his head. "Wasn't watching TV. Was thinkin' of goin' out for lunch."

"Isn't it kind of late for lunch?" Luther said, glancing at his watch. "It's almost four."

Hearing voices in the yard, Richard stepped outside. "Oh, it's you," he said.

"In the arborvitae," Elwood said pointedly. "I ain't eaten yet." He gestured toward Luther. "It's my lunchtime. You wanna join me?"

Luther looked at his watch again. "Well, I suppose it could be an early supper. Sure, I might as well."

Elwood grunted and looked at Luther. "You still eat Indian grub?" he said. "Pemmican and fry bread, chunks of maple sugar candy?"

"Good grief, Dad," Richard said.

Indians In The Arborvitae

Luther grinned. "Mr. Fundy, it isn't like that today. It's couscous, tabouli, tofu, curried shrimp, chevre quesadillas, porcini, and apple Betty. I dine on various and sundry comestibles. I have tried jerky, but I don't like it."

Elwood snorted. "Me neither." Then he told Luther he knew where they could get a swell dinner, and directed him to get into his Checker.

"Should I get in back?" Luther asked, chuckling.

"What for? Lotsa room up front. Dickie can sit in back." Elwood unlocked the driver's door, slid over and opened the passenger's side.

"Little joke," Luther said, easing in. "You know this is an old taxi, right? Passenger's supposed to sit in back?"

Elwood stared at him. Luther shrugged. "Never mind, Mr. Fundy. A weak attempt at humor." He clasped his hands behind his head and leaned back. "Where you taking me?"

Richard held Elwood's door open. "Dad, what's up? Where are you going?"

"Place you probably never been before. But I can guarantee the food's real good. Nothin' fancy, just awful darn good. You can even get seconds," he said, a smirk spreading across his face. "A few times, I've even got thirds."

Luther glanced at Elwood. "Thirds," he repeated. "Can't beat that. You coming, Rich?"

Richard coughed, groaned softly, and swung into the back seat. "Where we going, Dad?"

"You'll see," Elwood said, backing out of the driveway and turning onto County Road 114, then onto Lockling Road. He slowed briefly and turned to Luther. "Say, I've always wondered about this, but didn't know who to ask. You're a music man, though, so I'll ask you."

"Sure, be glad to try and help." Luther was looking at Elwood and resting his head against the passenger window.

"Well, sir, what happens to the music when the song ends?" Elwood swerved around a roadkill woodchuck.

Richard leaned forward in the back seat. "What do you mean, Dad?"

"Just what I said, Dickie. I read stuff, and I hear that things sort of go on forever. Like Steve Martin says about farts—they rise into the atmosphere and stay there as long as we got an ozone layer. You lose the ozone and all the farts from the beginning of time come falling back to earth. 'Course it'd kill practically everybody, wouldn't it? I guess I'd like to know if the same thing happens to music."

"What kind of question is that, Dad?"

Luther screwed up his face. "I never heard that about gas, Mr. Fundy, but I suppose it's plausible. Frankly, though, I never gave a thought about the ultimate end of music. It's an interesting question."

"Yes, I thought so," said Elwood, turning onto Prospect Avenue and heading into Cloquet. Finally, he halted the Checker in the parking lot of Faith of Enoch Lutheran Church. "Here we are," he said, grinning.

"A church, Mr. Fundy? What is this, a church supper?"

"Yeah, sort of."

Richard stepped out and noticed a hearse pulling away from the entrance. A man was carrying baskets of flowers back to the church. "Wait a minute, Dad," Richard said. "That's a hearse. This is a funeral, for crying out loud."

"Yeah, well it should be over by now. And it ain't only a funeral, boys. You oughta know there's always a lunch after."

Mouths open, Luther and Richard stood near the Checker as Elwood started for the church. "Mr. Fundy, those lunches are for the friends and family of the deceased," Luther said. "For people who actually went to the funeral."

"Hey, who's to know, Luther?" Elwood said, stepping forward, then turning back.

"Well, my dad could always spot funeral lunch crashers. He always made it a point to talk to them—you know, embarrass them a little."

"Yeah, well, your old man ain't here, Luther. Besides, a free lunch is a free lunch, far as I'm concerned."

Striding closer, Elwood shot a glance over his shoulder at the church. "I don't know how you boys vote, but I'm a lifelong Democrat. That weasel Nixon always said there's no such thing as a free lunch. The hell. Every lunch I don't pay for is free. Whenever there's a funeral, there's a free lunch, and if Nixon had been the sort of man who had friends, he'd have gone to funerals by God, and eaten some of those lunches. You take guys like me who're on fixed incomes. And you put on a funeral and throw in a free lunch, we're gonna go and eat." He paused for a moment, looking over the hood of the car at Luther and Richard. "You boys gonna eat or wait here?"

Luther walked slowly around the car. "What do you think, Rich? It's your call."

Shaking his head, Richard was leaning against the Checker. "We can't go in there, Dad. We didn't attend the funeral. Besides, who died?"

Elwood frowned. "One of the ladies from around town, I think. Can't remember her name. She's about 75-80." He turned. "Boys, we're gonna have to get in line. You don't want to be last otherwise you'll never get seconds."

"Or thirds," offered Luther.

"Damn right. Or thirds," Elwood said, laughing.

"Wait, Dad." Richard remained next to the Checker. "This isn't right."

"Then stay behind, Dickie. I'm gonna go in and eat." Luther looked at Richard, lifted his eyes and said, "Might as well, Rich."

As they ambled toward the church, Richard said, "Think real hard, Dad. Who passed away?"

"Like I said, some old dame about 75. But I could be wrong." Richard held Luther's arm, stopped and said he wasn't sure about going in and eating food prepared for mourners, especially since he hadn't mourned.

"Hey, mourning's easy," Elwood said. "You put on a long face and be real polite." Elwood continued walking, Luther a stride behind him. "I mean, who's gonna up and say you didn't know the deceased?"

"My dad would. He didn't speak well of funeral crashers." Luther caught up to Elwood and walked with him.

"We're just sharing the grief," Elwood said. "Nobody can begrudge a man sharing another's grief." He winked. "And, of course, sharing the chow." Hurrying to the door leading to the church basement, Elwood found himself at the end of a long line snaking out of the kitchen into hallways and classrooms. "If ya hadn't spent so much time yakking, Dickie, we'd of been up front, I betcha."

Seated at a long table in the basement, gumming quantities of cream of mushroom soup-based casseroles tasting faintly of Jell-O salad seepage, Elwood joined a discussion about one of the mourner's hiatal gas. The problem was, Elwood said, that elderly folks don't get enough fiber in their diets. "It don't help any that eating fiber can also give you some real bad gas. Now take me, for instance. Geez, I eat raw onions or baked beans, and right away my belly starts actin' up. Within an hour, I can clear out a room the size of this basement, if you know what I mean." He grimaced, and a man at the table, blinking rheumy blue eyes, nodded in agreement.

"Few years back, I was always checking my stools," Elwood continued. "When I was getting enough fiber, them stools floated right to the top of the bowl. When I wasn't, they sank like the Titanic."

"Oh my," an elderly woman remarked quietly, as conversation faded and people stood to fetch more coffee. "But now you've brought it up, the reason my Harvey isn't here is because he's embarrassed about his problem," she said, putting down her fork and lowering her voice. "Bladder control."

"Hey, he shouldn't be embarrassed. I mean, water happens. You get to a certain age, and water happens."

Luther nudged Elwood. "Maybe we shouldn't have this discussion here, you know?" he whispered.

Elwood grunted, and was silent a few moments before speaking again. "You ever notice when you get old you spend a lot of time frettin' about your bowels and hair in your ears? I know this one bald fella who's got so much hair in his ears he could run a brush through it. He could sweep all of it over the top of his head like a wig. No kidding."

"Dad," Richard said around a cough. He lowered his voice. "It's enough you crash a funeral luncheon without treating the guests to conversations about bodily functions."

Elwood tapped the shoulder of a man next to him. "I used to think when I was a young feller that life would be nothin' but roses once the boy grew up and left home. But it ain't been that way at all. The wife died eight years ago. Dickie divorced before he had any kids. So I got no grandchildren, and Dickie ain't the remarrying type. So the name dies out pretty quick. And Dickie, at 43 years-old, mind you, is living at home again. But what're ya gonna do? You can't leave 'em out in the cold. Kids," he added with a rueful shake of his head. The other man nodded uncomfortably, and gnawed on a wedge of cantaloupe.

It seemed the funeral was not for a 75 year-old woman, but rather an 81 year-old male named Marvin. One of the deceased's sons stopped by the table and thanked everyone for attending the service.

"Hey," said Elwood, wiping chocolate cake crumbs from the corners of his mouth, "it's the least a person can do for a good man. He'll be missed."

"He will," said the son. "Thank you so much."

Richard and Luther anxiously turned in their seats as the man passed by, resting his hand for a moment on Richard's shoulder. "Dad, I think it's time to go," Richard said, his face flushing.

Elwood put down his plastic fork and looked at Richard. "You're lucky, Luther, having the Indian complexion and all. You wanna see a man blush, you look at old Dickie. Reddern' a beet when he's embarrassed. And he's kinda dark himself. His mother used to say he was olive toned. But he always seemed a little dark to me, like them Eyetalians. Imagine how he'd blush if he had my skin. Hell, Luther—pardon my French—you could spend your whole life embarrassed and not a single soul would know it." He studied Luther's plate. "What's the matter with you—you've hardly touched your food."

Luther sighed then nudged Elwood. "I have to get out of here. There's a couple over there by the coffee urn who used to attend Veritas Unitarian in Floodwood—my dad's first church. They'll know I don't belong here." He and Richard stood.

"Yeah, well, I was startin' to have a pretty good time," Elwood said, "but okay."

In the parking lot Elwood unlocked the car. "Listen, the night's still young and I'm in the mood for a little bump. Whaddaya say?"

"I don't think so, Dad. I have papers to correct. I don't have time for hanging out in some saloon. And neither, I assume, does Luther."

"I don't know, Rich. I could stand a little nip."

"Well, okay," said Richard, scowling. "But let's not stay all night."

"I'll buy the drinks," Elwood said.

CHAPTER THREE

From the outside, on Chestnut Street, the saloon was a typical blue-collar haunt, situated in a neighborhood zoned for light industry. A single neon sign proclaimed ART'S PLACE in a script banner across the front. The bar occupied the ground floor of a three-story structure. The second floor housed a leather merchant specializing in hand-tooled belts, while two apartments were on the top floor. A small-engine repair business was situated on the east side of Art's Place, and a paper recycling firm occupied the adjacent west position.

Elwood parked the Checker across the street, and directed Luther and Richard to ignore the corner crosswalk and simply dash to the bar from the middle of the block.

Art's Place was well lighted, and a large Toulouse Lautrec poster depicting the interior of Maxim's greeted customers in the entry. A goldenrod flyer announcing a poetry slam was next to it. Several patrons greeted Elwood as he made his way to the interior of the bar and located a booth near the pool table, beneath prints by Jackson Pollock and Paul Klee. He removed his jacket and scanned the room. "Emil here yet?" he called to no one in particular. Then he hailed Arthur Fykes, the proprietor, who was putting bottles of Evian water into the cooler. "Artie, old man, when you're done there, jump over here. I want you to meet the associate conductor of the Duluth Symphony Orchestra, Luther Burgess-Durfee. He's with me and Dickie, who also happens to be my kid."

"Hi, guys." Arthur glanced at them and waved.

"Luther could fill everyone in on Scriabin. Remember that discussion we had last week? Used that chord of superposed fourths. Anyway, Luther knows the tunes, man," Elwood said, then ordered a Pernod and a pack of Wrigley's Spearmint. When

Arthur brought them over, Elwood nudged Richard. "Pay the man, Dickie, and order yourselves up a beer or some other poison."

"Beer's okay," Luther said.

"Yeah, I guess," added Richard.

While Arthur was drawing the brew, Elwood insinuated a wry smile. "Admit it, Artie, Marcel Duchamp could paint rings around Mark Rothko." He nudged Luther and Richard, whispering, "Arthur don't much care for the abstract expressionists."

Arthur nodded. "You may be right, Elwood."

"You damn betcha. That Rothko couldn't hold Duchamp's palette, Arthur. He couldn't even stretch his canvas." Elwood signaled Luther and chortled. The bartender merely sighed and strode to the jukebox, punching up a golden oldie—Robert Frost reading "Stopping by the Woods on a Snowy Evening." That quieted Elwood, who grunted and stared at his Pernod. Finally he spoke again. "See boys, what we have here is a very capable barkeep who just refuses to recognize Duchamp for what he did. Come here." Elwood stood and brought Luther and Richard through a jungle of potted ferns, stopping before a print of Duchamp's "Nude Descending a Staircase." "Thing is, Artie old man, is what Duchamp did with this. Lookie. You got successive phases of movement superimposed on each other."

"So?" said the bartender, now joining the others by the print. He was holding a glass of diet cola in his hand and a lighted curve-stemmed calabash between his teeth.

"You've got to respect the fact, Arthur, that old Duchamp initiated a dynamic version of facet Cubism."

"Facet Cubism?" Luther, smiling, looked at Richard who shrugged. "Facet Cubism," Richard repeated.

Arthur, grinning, glancing at Luther and Richard, allowed his hand to rest on Elwood's shoulder. As he was about to speak he was interrupted.

"Hey, Elwood—howsa boy?" Emil Slepka hadn't bothered to change his coveralls with MARTIN'S CHEVROLET in block letters on the back. "Lookin' at the Duchamp?" he said. "Forget him. I mean the guy was what, a flash in the pan? Now let's get serious here. Take George Bellows. There was a *real* artist, know what I mean? Look at this." He stood before one of Bellows' famous fight scenes, the one with Louis Firpo standing over Jack Dempsey after the champ had been knocked out of the ring. "Say, Arthur," he said without looking at the bartender. "I'd kinda like something sweet. I don't suppose you got any chocolate-chip cookies? Geez, bring me a couple of them and a Calvados."

"You got no taste, Emil. Your taste is down at the bottom of your shoes," said a woman seated at the bar. She was sipping a

Indians In The Arborvitae

Grand Marnier and smoking an unfiltered cigarette. "I used to be married to Barney 'The Kid' Campesi," she went on. "Remember him, Elwood? Arthur, you remember The Kid. Helluva fighter in his day. But you seen what happened to him—ended up scrambled." She made circles around her ear with her forefinger. "If he walked in here today, he wouldn't recognize a one of us, and that includes me."

"So, what're ya sayin', Irma?"

"That boxing ain't art, Emil. I don't care what nobody says, it ain't art."

"Hey, I agree, Irma," Elwood said. "Boxing ain't art; it's a science. They used to call it the sweet science. But this ain't the Science Saloon, is it? I don't think Arthur should have the Bellows in here neither. What I'd like is for there to be some Hans Arp or Max Ernst. And if need be, even a Joan Miro." He shrugged and nudged Luther. "Miro ain't too bad. He done what they called the biomorphic abstractions. Now there's a word for you, Arthur. Biomorphics. I betcha Dickie and Luther never heard that one before." He laughed. "Some day we ought to have a discussion on biomorphics, know what I mean? Anyhow, them designs of Miro's were curvilinear, fluid. Hey, he knew what to do with his brush, that guy."

Luther and Richard exchanged looks of astonishment, as Elwood was saying, "Same as old Chopin knew what to do with his piano."

"Chopin, Chopin, Chopin." Irma scoffed. "Can't you get off that track, Elwood? He's so ... derivative."

"Hey, why is everybody here so hung up on classical music? Don't nobody here dig jazz? Thelonius Monk, Teddy Wilson—them guys played a helluva piano." A man in housepainter's coveralls hummed a few bars of ''Round Midnight,' then nodded at Elwood. "You're probably not the right guy to talk to about jazz, Elwood, but if truth be told, I find a lot of pretension in this classical crap."

"You don't like it, Hoskar, because you're into the so-called cool school," Elwood said. "You're afraid to just be yourself and appreciate the totality of musical expression."

Hoskar carried his brandy Manhattan over to Elwood's booth. Elwood shook his hand and introduced him to Richard and Luther. "Hoskar's an artiste," he said, grinning. "Conceptual. Works with concrete. And he's due our congratulations. I heard you just got a commission from the local playground association to fashion something or other."

Hoskar nodded. A gray-haired, barrel-shaped man with thick, rough-callused hands, he took off his dust-covered baseball cap and thwacked it against his thigh. "Yeah. I'll put down a few basement blocks and see what happens. You can't turn down your nose at a $20,000 commission. I hope accepting it don't compromise my artistic integrity." He put his hand on Elwood's shoulder. "Listen, when I get down to it, maybe you wanna come over and heft some blocks for me. I pay pretty good, and Irma said she'd bring over a thermos of martinis." Elwood said he'd think about it.

Robert Frost was still having miles to go before he slept, and Emil didn't want to hear any more. He said he was going to play some selections from Allen Ginsberg's "Howl." Or maybe some music would change the mood in the place, he suggested.

"Come off it, Emil," Irma said. "Not that baldy, Ginsberg. Gimme some Dylan Thomas. Actually, I could go for some Samuel Barber or old Philip Glass."

"When it's your coins you can have a say, Irma," Emil said.

"Arthur," Elwood was saying to the bartender, "getting back to this Bellows picture. I have to wonder if it really belongs anymore. I mean, the thing is, if art ain't political, what is it? It's gotta mean something."

"That's telling him, Elwood," Irma said.

Arthur sighed and lighted Irma's fresh cigarette. "Everybody's entitled to an opinion," he said quietly. "But at the very least it represents history, if not art. I mean Hemingway boxed, Pound boxed. A. J. Liebling boxed and wrote some wonderful stuff about boxing. For all I know, Picasso may have boxed. The Bellows stays." He looked at Richard and Luther. "What do you boys think?"

"I can't fathom this," Luther said, grinning. "I mean look at this place. How did you ever get these people interested in art and music? This is absolutely incredible. There's nothing at all like this down in Duluth—the one in Georgia. And I bet there's nothing like this in the Minnesota Duluth either."

"Incredible," Richard said. "This is totally surreal."

"Salvador Dali was the surrealist, Dickie," his father said, before facing Arthur. "I know this is your place, Art, but I'm gonna level with you. You got your Bellows here, you might just as well get yourself a collection of them Norman Rockwell baseball pictures. And then, Arthur, once you start bringin' in Norman Rockwell, what's to stop you from hangin' some Walter Keane?" He guffawed. "How 'bout one of them cutesy little kitties with great big eyes, and maybe the kitty could be wearin' a baseball cap. Now we're talkin' first-rate, world-class."

Emil stiffened. "Hey, nobody said nothin' about Rockwell or Keane," he said, adding somewhat belligerently. "You impugnin' my good taste, Elwood?"

"Why shore," said Elwood, his inhibitions loosened by Pernod. "You're nothin' but a closet Keane freak." He laughed.

Emil, who was several years younger than Elwood, though a half-foot shorter, stepped toward him with a cocked fist. "You better take that back, Elwood. You and me been friends a lotta years, but nobody calls me a Keane freak, includin' you."

"Dad," Richard said, rising, attempting to step between Elwood and Emil. Luther also stood, signaling Arthur who was mixing a Pimm's Cup for another regular.

"Hey, whoa," said Irma, leaving her barstool and approaching the booth. "It's none of my business, but if you ask me, old Elwood's dead right."

"Well nobody asked you, Irma," Emil retorted. "So you just mind your own business, because this has got nothin' to do with you."

At that moment a small entourage came through the door. "That's Stan Armbrister and the boys," Elwood said to Richard and Luther. "Works down at the sanitation department." He leaned across the table, whispering confidentially,"He's had a thing for Irma here for quite a while."

"This Edna Ferber groupie givin' you a hard time, Irma?" Stan said, dropping his lunch bucket on the bar.

"Hey, Edna Ferber was a beautiful writer," Emil said. *So Big* was a helluva movie. You don't see 'em makin' lotsa films out of James Joyce, do you? 'Course not. How you gonna get that interior stuff on the screen?"

Stan snorted. "You think great literature is measured by how many movies get made out of somebody's novels?" He laughed and nudged Irma, who smiled coyly.

Arthur Fykes, meanwhile, uneasy with the disquieting tension in his establishment, stepped forward. "Hey, everybody," he called out. "Let's not let our passion for the arts overrun our good senses. Look, I got some new stuff for the jukebox. What say we listen to some vintage John Berryman doing his rendition of a few *Dream Songs?* Now Berryman was our kind of guy, right? Hell of a drinker and hell of a poet. How about we give him a listen?"

"He's a creep, a misogynist," Irma hollered.

"I say, let's hear him," Emil shouted.

"I second whoever's right" Elwood said, and giggled before downing another Pernod.

"Dad, maybe we should leave," Richard suggested. "Luther, you ready?"

"No, Rich. This is fantastic."

Stan was in Emil's face now, threatening to rearrange his proboscis.

"Go ahead, Stan," Emil said, standing his ground. "You've been wanting to for a long time now. Go ahead, be a big shot." He jutted his jaw toward Stan.

Stan calmly lifted Irma's drink, put it to his lips, and took some in his mouth. Then he turned back toward Emil and showered him with the Grand Marnier. Stan cleared his throat while Emil, blinking and squinting to keep the alcohol from his eyes, groped for a handkerchief. "If Emil chooses, he may retaliate," Stan began. "However, I have considered what I did for a long time now. I am familiar with the need for artists to process their work. When I spit on Emil it was part of a process. I mean, it was more to make an artistic statement than it was to hurt Emil, though I admit that if Emil didn't like it, so much the better."

Arthur handed Emil a clean towel, and Emil mopped his face. "Waste of good liquor, Stan," he said evenly.

"If he done that to me," said Hoskar, "I'd bury him in a ton of cement."

Elwood stood. "I liked it, Stan," he said. "Think of it, Emil; Stan may have resurrected the Dada movement. Look at it this way, Stanley. In the old days when you and the boys would go down to Rockland Castle and pick fights with those hairballs from Crosier County, you'd end up in jail for disturbing the peace. You could go down there now and just slap the snot out of them and tell the cops you wasn't fightin' at all, just doin' Dada art. I love it."

"It ain't so bad, I suppose," said Emil somewhat glumly. "If you ain't on the receivin' end of a kick."

Everyone laughed then; bonhomie returned to Art's Place, and Arthur Fykes set up drinks all around, on the house. He inserted several quarters into the antique Wurlitzer, and hoisted his own Cinzano cocktail. "To peaceful, passionate discourse," he said. "To Rimbaud, Rauschenberg and Man Ray."

"Hear, hear," chorused the patrons, glasses raised, arms around each other's shoulders, Ezra Pound's inscrutable *Cantos* playing on the jukebox.

"See, what'd I tell you boys," Elwood said. "Wonderful little establishment Arthur has here. And I believe I learn more here in a month than you could teach me at Harvard."

As Luther was shaking his head, Richard felt a hand on his shoulder. Glancing up, he saw the taped glasses and beaming round face of his principal, Hulot Piquete. "Fundy," said Dr. Piquete, appearing out of character in a cashmere turtleneck sweater and beret. "Fancy finding you here."

Blushing, Richard stood. "Dr. Piquete. This is a surprise. I should introduce you to my father, Elwood Fundy." Richard placed his hand on his father's shoulder. "And my friend, Luther Burgess-

Durfee."

Still smiling broadly, Dr. Piquete vigorously pumped Elwood's hand. "Hulot Pique," he said. "Principal at Button Gwinnet. We're just awfully impressed with your son's work, Mr. Fundy," he said.

"It's good to hear that Dickie knows something that impresses an educated man. His late mother and me always hoped that putting him through college would pay off in the end."

Dr. Piquete turned his attention to Luther. "And I've heard of you, sir," he said, taking Luther's hand. "Your reputation precedes you in this neck of the woods." He glanced at Richard. "So you two are friends?"

"We went to high school together," Luther said. "I'm back here on a sabbatical."

"So I've heard," Dr. Piquete said. "Read something about it in the Sanguine Society newsletter. Your father was a Sanguinoid, isn't that right? Seems to me I met him quite a few years ago when I first joined the Button Gwinnet family. So how's he enjoying his retirement? Reverend Durfee still down in Florida?"

"Yes." Luther nodded.

Dr. Piquete scratched his chin, dissolving his smile. He told the three that he wasn't in the habit of pub-crawling or indeed, visiting taverns and saloons of any stripe, but that Art's Place was distinctive. "One of the few places on God's green earth where one finds the cultural heritage of a community so vastly nurtured and enriched." He glanced at the pilsners before Richard and Luther. "I don't imbibe myself, but Arthur Fykes has seen fit to order in a stash of ginger beer, which is my beverage of choice. You gentlemen ever try ginger beer?"

Elwood pointed his index finger into his mouth and made a gagging sound. Frowning, Richard covered Elwood's hand with his own and pressed it against the table.

"Yes, well I suppose it takes a little getting used to," Dr. Piquete said through a strained smile. "I'm of the old school, gentlemen. A school administrator ought not imbibe alcohol, and certainly not in public. One even hesitates to be seen in such an establishment, heh-heh. Hence this little disguise, if you catch my drift."

"I catch your drift," said Luther, and Dr. Piquete turned to him. "It behooves me to make inquiry of you, Mr. Burgess-Durfee. I know both you and Fundy are graduates of the Luffington High School, and I've heard nothing but excellent reports about the place. But I wonder if it might not be possible for you to come over to Button Gwinnet some time and talk to our music students and staff. I know it would mean the world to them. And you might wish to know that Fundy *fis* here, has been most efficacious in heightening community awareness about Button Gwinnet, the man for whom our school is named."

"We might arrange for that," Luther said. "But I wouldn't want to compete with Rich's talk on the old Button, whose name still resonates a bit down in Georgia." He smiled.

Hulot Piquete pinched his lips together before responding. "Education isn't competitive at Button Gwinnet, Mr. Burgess-Durfee. Education is always enlightening, always edifying. There's nothing in the least bit competitive about it—at least not at our school. I don't know how it may have been at Luffington Senior High."

"It was edifying," Richard said.

Elwood signaled for a pilsner and side shot. "Wasn't either, Dickie," he said. "Maybe it was for Luther 'cause he was valedictorious. But you didn't seem to get many hills of beans out of it. You wasn't very active in high school, Dickie. I'da hoped you'd maybe of played on the football team, or done some wrestling. A father likes to see his son do manly things like that. But it wasn't your style, or somethin'. When I think about football, now that's about the only time I have to hand it to old Tricky Nixon."

"Oh, and how is that?" Hulot Piquete pulled up a chair and sat.

"Well, sir, there just wasn't all that much to him, but he wants to play ball with these big tough guys. He's no bigger'n Dickie here, and probably not even that big. So they put him out there at defensive end, and of course the bruisers just crash into him play after play, drive him into the dirt, smash him upside and downside till he probably wishes he lined up offside. I mean everybody just wipes up the ground with this scrawny, mealy-mouthed Nixon. I mean nobody back then would of given you a tinker's damn about his chances of getting elected President or anything else for that matter. But see, he persisted. Got knocked down and had your nose busted, he gets up again and gets a bloody lip or sprained ankle. Just won't quit. Man couldn't play football, and he couldn't play President either, but by God, he wouldn't quit. And I'm forced to admire that. Truth be told, I wish Dickie had of been more like Nixon when it came to gettin' knocked to hell and gone. As it is, the only thing they had in common was the first name."

"Well now, Mr. Fundy, you'd have to search pretty far and wide to find a bigger sports fan than yours truly," said Dr. Piquete. "However, athletics are not the be-all and end-all that many believe. Your son is a scholar, sir, and there are precious few of them in society."

Elwood nodded at the waitress who brought his drinks, and he quickly downed the shot. "I am not a man of formal education, Mr. Piquete," he said. "But what good is a scholar who can't fix a carburetor? Who can't dig up arborvitae when they hide certain

Indians who spy on his father's house? I don't mean you, Luther," he added quickly. "If that's a scholar, Mr. Piquete, I ask you, what's a poor, struggling father to do?"

"Appreciate him, Mr. Fundy," Dr. Piquete said, resting his hand on Richard's shoulder. "Appreciate him for what he is, for what he does, as I do, sir." He paused, glancing into the faces of the others in the booth. Appreciate and—yes, uphold such a man, lest he find himself bereft. Now as for the arborvitae, I know your son will take care of them. Won't you, Fundy?"

"Dr. Piquete, I..." said Richard, flushing, turning away.

Dr. Piquete glanced at his watch. "Golly, time flies, doesn't it, gentlemen? It's soon ten o'clock, and tomorrow's another day. I don't know about you folks, but Fundy and I are expected to be at school tomorrow morning bright eyed and bushy tailed. We require our rest. And as you may have heard, every hour of sleep before midnight is worth two after." He smiled. "In any case, I'm heading for hearth and home. I expect you won't be long yourself, hey, Fundy? Got to get your beauty sleep."

"Of course," Richard said. "My beauty sleep."

Elwood, put down his drink. "You think Dickie's handsome, Piquete?"

Dr. Piquete laughed. "I meant that as a figure of speech, Mr. Fundy, but on—"

"He's an average looking guy, wouldn't you say? Sorta like the old man, don't you think?" Elwood smoothed his hair and rolled his tongue over his teeth. He smiled.

"Hey, you're a regular matinee idol, Mr. Fundy," Luther said. "But Rich resembles his mother—at least as I remember her."

Elwood frowned. "Yeah, he always did take after her."

"To answer your question directly, Mr. Fundy, there's absolutely nothing at all wrong with the way your son looks," said Dr. Piquete. He glanced at his watch again. "Golly, this has been fun. We must meet here again sometime. Enjoyed meeting you gentlemen." As he started for the door, he turned back. "Bright and early, Fundy," he called, making his way to the front door.

Elwood followed him with his eyes, then lifted his drink again. "Man seems to care about you, your health and so forth, Dickie," he said. "Still he's got this pee-head quality about him, if you know what I mean."

Luther chuckled; Richard stared at his pilsner. "He's right, though, Dad. We should be leaving now. I have a full day tomorrow."

Elwood nodded, and indicated Richard should pay for the final round of drinks.

As they were getting into the Checker, Elwood said that maybe he should have gone to the men's room first. "But we'll be home in a jiffy," he said. "I'll be okay."

The route back to Mister Lane had been detoured by night crews repairing a breach in the water main. Elwood was forced to take meandering side streets before arriving at the crest of Fern Avenue where a long, gradual descent brought it to 144th Street.

"No traffic behind us is there, Dickie?" Elwood said, slowing and pulling off to the side.

"No, why?" Richard said, glancing out the rear window. "What're we stopping for?"

"Can't wait, Dickie. Gotta take a leak."

Elwood bounded from the car and unzipped his trousers. He retreated behind the car. "You boys have to go too? Nobody's around."

"Geez, Dad," Richard moaned. But Luther also left the car and joined Elwood. Richard emerged from the back of the car. "You guys," he said, shaking his head as the two men urinated.

Suddenly, the car began to move. "Dad! The car!" Richard hollered, as the Checker rolled down the slope.

"Stop her, Dickie," his father yelled, giving chase. Richard froze, and the car, followed by the unzipped, appendage-loosed Elwood, continued its descent. Luther, urinating, looked after the scene, transfixed.

The Checker seemed not to gain speed, yet stayed several paces ahead of Elwood, who was unable to catch it as it approached the bottom of the slope, heading into a long left curve. As the Checker began banking left, another car heading in the opposite direction rammed it head-on. Elwood, catching up to his car, ran into the stopped Checker and flew over the roof, landing on the hood, where he rolled off onto the pavement.

The other driver was quickly outside, standing over Elwood and trembling, "Are you all right? Please, God, are you all right?"

Elwood slowly got to his feet, unaware of his exposed member, and rubbed his shins. "I'm okay," he mumbled.

Richard and Luther hurried to the scene as the other driver was explaining the accident. "This was incredible," he said. "I don't know what happened. It seemed like just a little tap, but this gentleman was tossed from his car onto the hood and he fell off right here." The man indicated the spot. "Musta tore his fly open on the side mirror," he added, staring. "Geez, look at that."

Elwood tucked himself in and closed the zipper.

Luther pulled Richard away as the men examined their vehicles and exchanged insurance information. As the other man drove off, Elwood signaled Richard and Luther. "Not a word, Dickie," he said. "I don't want to hear one damned word about this."

"You won't, Mr. Fundy," Luther said. "Hell, it could happen to anyone."

"Yeah, I know."

"No, Dad, it could not happen to anyone. It's never happened to anyone ever before. Not like this. You made history tonight. That was careless, idiotic even. You don't run after a car with your...*tool* flapping in the breeze. People get arrested for that alone. Urinating on public property also carries a fine, I'm sure, to say nothing of public humiliation when your name is in the papers."

"I said not a word, Dickie, and I meant it," Elwood said. "You listen to your father."

"You sure you're all right, Mr. Fundy?" Luther said.

"Bruises on my legs," Elwood remarked sourly. "First time I ever been in an accident like this. You don't think that other fella seen anything, do you?"

"Yes, and I'm sure there could be hell to pay too, Dad. You embarrassed the other driver and caused that accident."

"A man's gotta go when he's gotta go, Dickie." Elwood turned around and spoke directly to his son. "Now, enough. Not another word. Let's go home."

"This would have just killed Mom," Richard said.

Elwood sighed. "Your mother's already dead, Dickie. Let's just drop it."

Richard often thought of his mother these days. Moreso even than in the weeks and months following her death. The spruce at the bottom of the hill reminded him of his childhood when Rae would sit in the rocker at Christmastime, watching the tree lights blink on and off. She'd be listening to a recording of Fred Waring's Pennsylvanians' "The Night Before Christmas," and eat up to a half-dozen clementines. His father would be in the den, cursing a televised football game, urging Richard to watch with him. Occasionally he'd holler at Rae to stop eating so many clementines. They'd give her the trots, and she'd be sorry. Sometimes, she would venture into the TV room and plop down on the sofa next to her husband, rest her hand on his knee and ask what he might like for dinner. "Send out for pizza. Pepperoni and onions."

Richard, meanwhile, passed the holiday time trying to assemble toys and kits left by Santa. As he grew older, he skated at Emory Park rink, not a quarter mile from the house. It was good, he used to think, to be out of the house at Christmas, when his mother would first pine for, then eat, boxes of clementines, and as his dad predicted, develop the trots.

There had been a melancholy to his parents' lives together; he often felt his father seemed happier now without Rae. Though last Christmas, Elwood bought a box of clementines and put them under the tree. He said he didn't want Richard eating them. Just before New Year's, they were gone. Richard hadn't seen Elwood eat them but they were gone.

Richard's reverie was broken by the braking of the Checker in the Fundy driveway.

"Here we are," Elwood said.

"Dad, we should take Luther home."

Luther shook his head. "I'll walk, Rich. It isn't far."

"You heard the man, Dickie. Isn't far." Elwood turned off the engine, grabbed the keys and headed for the house.

"Dickie!" Elwood shouted, bursting into Richard's bedroom shortly before six a.m. How come you never told me I had all this hair in my ears?"

Richard rubbed his eyes and sat up. "Huh? What are you talking about, Dad?"

His father had thumbs and forefingers inserted in both ears, pinching sworls of gray hairs. "I got hair in my own ears, Dickie," he cried, agitated. "How come you never said nothin'? I mean there I was at the funeral yesterday, talkin' about how old geezers get hair in their ears, and I'm sittin' there with a whole buncha hair in my own ears, and my so-called son sits there with me, and doesn't say a damn word. You embarrassed me, Dickie. I can't understand it."

Richard moaned and eased his legs over the side of the bed. He rubbed his eyes again.

"That's it, Dickie, rub 'em. Rub 'em good, 'cause you sure don't see much."

"Dad, it's no big deal. So what? You've got hair in your ears. So do most men your age."

"Ohhhhh," Elwood groaned. "Listen, Dickie, remember that night back when you were in high school? You was set to take off for a date or something, but I seen you had this big ugly goober in your beak? Did I just let you go off with that thing? I did not. I informed you."

"I remember," Richard said quietly. "You told me in front of my friends, in a real loud voice, and then you laughed. Some favor."

Elwood tugged on his ear hairs. "Yeah, but I said something. You—you say nothing at all. I'm supposed to meet some friends for lunch tomorrow, Dickie, but I can't go out lookin' like this, for cryin' out loud."

"What do you want me to do about it?" Richard stood and looked around for his underwear, which he'd left hanging on the bedpost.

Indians In The Arborvitae

"They got them clippers 'specially for ear and nose hair. You can get 'em at the drug store. I want you to stop and buy me one on your way home from school. And make it snappy." Fingers in his ears, Elwood turned and left.

Richard leaned forward and turned off the clock radio, set to sound in 20 minutes, and leaned back against his pillow. He stared into his closet, and wondered if he had any clean shirts. He'd forgotten to pick up a batch from the cleaners. He sighed, got out of bed and went to the closet, selecting a shirt he'd worn on Tuesday.

Downstairs, Elwood sat in front of the television, watching cartoons and eating a bowl of Captain Crunch. He hollered as Richard went into the kitchen, "Don't eat all the sugar bombs, Dickie. There's not much left, and I'll probably want another bowl this morning."

Richard drank a glass of Tang and made instant coffee from the kitchen tap. He grabbed his briefcase and headed out.

"Don't forget them clippers, Dickie. I'll be real disgusted if you do," Elwood called after him.

Chapter Four

Richard arrived at school nearly an hour before classes began and helped himself to a cup of coffee from the urn in the faculty lounge. He sat at the table across from Adrian LaGrande, a biology instructor, who was grading test papers. LaGrande peered over the top of his reading glasses at Richard and shook his head. "Gets worse every year," he said, dropping his red pencil on the stack of papers.

"Yes?" Richard said.

"Wait'll you've been here a while, then you'll understand." LaGrande said. "Here, look at these." He extracted a couple of tests from the pile already corrected, and shoved them toward Richard. "Look at the answer there on number 14. The question was to describe the functions of the human skeletal system. Where are these kids' minds?" He shook his head.

Richard took one of the papers. A ninth grade boy had responded to the question: "The main use of the skeletal system is so we won't fall in a heap." The other response was: "Our skeletal system holds the meat on our bones." Richard smiled and pushed the papers back to LaGrande.

"Well," Richard said, "they aren't exactly wrong. Kind of funny, actually."

LaGrande frowned. "I suppose you're right. At least they had a notion. Half these kids didn't have the foggiest. Old Stew Thompson—he's retired now—once showed me an answer a kid wrote in his history class. The question was how did the Medieval Church raise money? The kid said, paper drives and bake sales." LaGrande grunted. "I dunno, pal. I don't know if I can do this another 15 years before I can retire. And you, Fundy—you're just starting out."

"Oh, it isn't all that bad."

"Yeah, well it doesn't hurt that Piquete thinks your sweat doesn't stink."

"What are you talking about?"

"Piquete's always had this bug up his butt about Button Gwinnet, and apparently you're the one who's the authority on the Button. I'd say you got it made, buddy. Piquete can be a real jerk when he doesn't like someone. So anyway, is everything all right these days with you?"

Richard nodded. "Fine, why?"

LaGrande studied Richard for a moment. "Oh, no reason. I'd heard you'd been having trouble with Indians out at your place. That right? Anyhoo, I just wondered how things were going."

Richard smiled. "It's not me, actually, it's my dad. He thinks Indians are hiding behind his arborvitae and spying on his house." He chuckled. "I more or less attribute it to his age."

Adrian pushed his glasses back on the bridge of his nose. "I don't know, Rich, the old guy could be right. You ever consider that?"

Richard was about to laugh, but observed Adrian's serious countenance, and resisted. "I don't think so," he said.

Hilda Narr entered the lounge and inserted a dollar into the Coke machine. She popped the can and brought it to the table, sighing as she settled on a chair. "Well, Richard Fundy," she started brightly after taking a long swallow of soda. "How goes the battle?"

"Fine."

"He's fine, Hilda," LaGrande said.

"That's not exactly what I hear from Dr. Piquete, Adrian," Hilda said, covering a burp with her hand.

"Good grief, Hilda, I'm fine—just fine," Richard said sharply, blushing.

Adrian LaGrande drummed his pencil on the table and looked from Richard to Hilda. "Is there something I don't know here? We were just talking about his dad having problems with Indians sneaking around the property, and I said to give the old man credit. You can't be too careful these days."

"It's nothing, Adrian." Richard said.

Hilda smiled. "I'm not so sure, Richard. I don't know anything about the Native American issue, and frankly, that's not my concern. I'm to oversee the health and welfare of our students, and by extension, our faculty. But Richard here presents something of a challenge because he is heartsick."

"Huh? Heartsick? What do you mean, heartsick?"

"Dammit, Hilda—"

"From lack of succor," Hilda said, shrugging.

Adrian looked from Hilda to Richard. "What's succor?"

"Please Hilda. Just forget it, okay?"

She reached across the table and patted Richard's hand. "Dr. Piquete defines it as nurture, comfort—that sort of thing," said Hilda, smiling. "Poor dear."

"You guys are joking, right?" Adrian snorted and rolled his eyes. "Who in hell among us gets nurtured and comforted? I mean, we walk into a zoo every day and toss peanuts to the monkeys. They sink or swim with 'em, far as I'm concerned. Comes the day I gotta nurture and comfort them, is the day the school board can kiss my ass."

"My, aren't we anal-retentive today, Adrian," Hilda said. "While Richard's situation isn't grave, it could be serious, and we're talking about him, not his students." She leaned forward, smiling a gap-toothed smile. "I don't know how this will sit with you, Adrian, but it could be invaluable to Richard and other teachers in the same boat. Yesterday Dr. Piquete asked me to look into arranging a district-wide workshop on appropriate ways to nurture faculty and staff. Our environment must be conducive to a climate where the Button Gwinnet family can be open and express themselves, and can share their hurts and anguishes, Dr. Piquete says."

"What?" Adrian stood.

Richard held his head in his hands. Hilda walked around the table and placed her hand on his shoulder. "You see, Mr. Fundy, it isn't only you. There are others among our little family who struggle with anxiety and depression, who feel unworthy, unloved, inadequate, untrustworthy, inexplicably irritable, prone to fits of pique, given to shirking responsibilities, which leads to ineffectual classroom teaching. Those are Dr. Piquete's words. Now speaking as a health care professional, what do we call these poor souls, Adrian?"

Mouth agape, Adrian LaGrande blinked. "I bet you know the answer to that one, Hilda."

She smiled. "We call them sick, Adrian. And in my professional judgment, sick people are seeking cures. How many billions do you suppose are spent researching cancer or heart disease, or AIDS?"

"Geez, I have no idea, Hilda," Adrian said.

"Neither do I. But I do know this—there's not one thin dime being spent on the all-too-common afflictions such as those endured by our Mr. Fundy, and the impact it thrusts upon the school environment. Instead of making light of Richard's problem, we should be thanking him for bringing it to our collective attention. He had the courage to confront his demons and to make them public."

"I did not make them public, Hilda," Richard shouted.

"He brought it to the attention of certain individuals who were in a position to take action." Hilda touched Richard's hand, but he pulled away. "I know we'll get to the bottom of this, Richard, and you'll be yourself again in no time at all."

"So, there's nothing wrong with your heart then, Richard?" Adrian solicited.

"Oh my, no. He suffers not physical pain, but rather a profound spiritual anguish, isn't that right?" Hilda drained the rest of her soft drink in two long gulps.

Adrian gathered his papers. "Geez, I'm sorry about your problem, Rich. But it doesn't seem life-threatening. Hang in there, buddy." He glanced at the wall clock as the buzzer sounded, signaling five minutes until first period classes would start.

Hilda crushed the Coke can and tossed it into a recycling receptacle 10 feet distant. "Narr hits a three!" she shouted, and pumped her fist. Chuckling, she turned back to Richard who had not moved from his chair. "It really isn't so bad," Hilda said. "We're all pulling for you, and looking to get things fixed right. So don't you worry one bit."

Richard didn't look at her, and felt a hand on his shoulder. He turned and looked up into the delicately aged face of Mildred Hoppe, one of Button Gwinnet's Home Economics teachers. "You listen to Hilda, young man, and I guarantee things will work out in the end. They just always do around here. We take good care of one another at Button Gwinnet. One person's problems quickly become another's and so on and so forth. It's terribly uplifting. I certainly am pulling for you. You can count on practically everyone in this room. What am I saying? You can count on everyone in this whole school, Mr. Fundy." She stepped back to look in her mailbox and spoke to Hilda. "Say, did you read that article in *Competitive Quilting* that I put in your box last week? They say they're going to try to get quilting listed as an Olympic sport. Now if that isn't something. After I retire from teaching, if ever I do, I could become an Olympic athlete." She chuckled. "My, wouldn't that be something."

"You'd look terrific in Olympic sweats, Mildred," Adrian said.

"Indeed she would," said Hilda.

"Quilting?" Adrian said. In the Olympics? Somebody's gone flat off his rocker."

"Her rocker," corrected Hilda. "Quilting International's secretary general is a woman. But on the other hand, it makes perfect sense to me. I mean, I like ice dancing as well as the next fellow, but if that's a sport, why not quilting?"

"Oh come on," Adrian roared. "I agree ice dancing isn't a sport, but quilting? My grandma was a quilter, but she was no athlete, I can tell you. And why stop there? How about baton twirling, or bridge and 500?"

"Well," Mildred Hoppe said, "it certainly is something to ponder."

"It isn't either," Adrian said. "It the stupidest thing I ever heard of, don't you think, Rich? I tell you what it is, folks, the damned feminization of our culture, that's what I think. What do you say, Rich?"

Richard's head was on the table, cradled in his crossed arms.

"Are you feeling all right?" Hilda asked and felt his forehead. "Oooh, you're a little warm. Come down to the office with me and let me take your temperature. You might be coming down with the flu or something. If so, you should be home in bed, not exposing others to whatever it is you've got."

Richard stood. "I'll be okay," he said weakly.

"Uh-uuh." Hilda shook her head. "You either come and let me have a look, or I tell Dr. Piquete you're insisting on teaching your class while ill. I'll examine your throat too. Lots of strep going around school right now." She held the lounge door open for Richard.

❖❖❖❖❖

As he turned onto Mister Lane after school, Richard saw his father at the edge of the driveway holding a spade. He was mopping his brow with a handkerchief and stepped out of the way as Richard pulled in. He had dug up the arborvitae. There was a 20-foot long trench wherehe had wrested the shrubs from the soil. Richard got out of his car and Elwood lit a cigarette.

"See what I done, Dickie?" Elwood gestured toward the trench. "Dug 'em up. No more arborvitae and no more Indians either, thank God." He leaned against his shovel and groaned. "Yeah, some action was necessary here, seein' as how you wasn't about to take care of 'em like I asked."

Richard frowned. "You know I'd have gotten to them eventually, Dad. I hoped you'd leave them in. Looks kind of naked now."

"That's the point, Dickie. Naked. Naked can't hide nothin'. So, anyway, that should take care of the Indian problem. Bet Luther'll be surprised."

"I suppose." Richard wandered over to look at the trench. "I'll go in and change, then fill this in for you."

"Durn tootin' you will, Dickie. You know this is just the sort of work puts a terrible strain on my heart. I'm gonna have to go lie down for a while. Supper's on your head tonight, Dickie. Maybe you'll fix pot roast. I got one thawin' on the kitchen table. Pot roast, boiled spuds, gravy—maybe open a can of beets. Oh, and when you finish fillin' in the trench, run down to Overmeier's Bakery and get a couple loaves of that oatmeal bread. I like it, and it's supposed to be good for the heart." He flicked his cigarette into the trench and watched it smolder for several seconds. "I'm bushed, Dickie. Wake me for dinner." He ambled toward the house.

Richard went inside, slipped out of his sport coat and slacks, and put on blue jeans and a sweatshirt. He put the roast in the oven before going outside again, where he spent the next hour filling in the arborvitae trench. He made the trip to the bakery, purchased the bread his father requested, and then returned home to peel potatoes in the kitchen that was still his mother's. The *Saturday Evening Post* cover print of Norman Rockwell's Thanksgiving dinner was still taped to the refrigerator door after nearly 35 years. Her floral patterned pan holders lay on the decorative cutting board where no meat or vegetables or bread had ever been sliced. The enamel sun-yellow paint had darkened to a thin beige, highlighted by a cloud of grease on the ceiling above the kitchen fan that Elwood never bothered to turn on.

Elwood, barefoot, joined Richard in the kitchen. "Couldn't sleep, Dickie." He opened the refrigerator and withdrew a bottle of beer. "I been thinkin', Dickie, about what's to become of me."

"What do you mean, Dad?"

Elwood sipped beer and burped. "I mean after I'm gone." He paused and looked at Richard, anticipating a response. Richard continued peeling potatoes. "After I'm dead, Dickie. I'm up there in bed thinkin' what's to be done."

Richard glanced at his father while placing potatoes in a pan of water. "Hey, you sure you want to talk about this now? I mean, I assumed you'd have a funeral like everybody else, and we'd bury you next to Mom."

Scowling, Elwood stared out the window above the sink. "I been thinkin' I don't want that. I want something different. You might not think so, but I'm a creative guy, Dickie. Don't laugh."

"I'm not, Dad. Go on."

"I want to be cremated. Burn the old bod to a crisp. I was watchin' this infomercial on TV the other day, and it made me wanna puke. This mortician was on hustlin' his mortuary—got a slew of 'em all over the country. Anyway, if you can picture this, he's got this dead guy layin' out on the table there, and he talks about embalming and all that stuff. Even shows us what happens when you expire. Expire's his word, Dickie, not mine.

"So he takes this kinda knifey tool and jabs the guy in the groin, right next to the old gazoons. That's where they drain the blood, he says. Well, a few more minutes of that and I seen all I cared to. None of that for me, I'm thinkin'. So I'm just gonna go for cremation. Seems a whole lot better than rottin' in some expensive casket under the ground."

"Fine, Dad, if that's what you want." Richard scanned the cupboard for a can of beets, extracted one and wiped the top before opening it.

Elwood nodded. "Been thinkin' about the music too. I ain't much for that churchy stuff, Dickie. Music, I mean. I thought about Chopin, who I like a great deal, but I'd sorta like something bigger. Grieg, who was a Norske, for your information, has a good piece I'd like played—that there Mountain King song."

"Well, it's your funeral, Dad. That'll surprise folks, for sure."

"I always liked surprises, Dickie. I remember when I was a little kid, and when your grandparents would go out for dinner or on a trip, I'd always ask them to bring me home a surprise. They mostly did—candy, funny books, you know. I always liked surprises. Until I got old. Then there are certain surprises a fella don't need."

"Yeah, like what?"

Elwood struck a wooden match and lit a cigarette. He was not looking at Richard, and seemed not to have heard him. "But Grieg would give everybody a surprise. A sort of fun surprise, know what I mean?" He looked at Richard. "That okay with you, Dickie?"

Richard nodded, and helped himself to a beer.

"Then there's one other thing. I always liked jokes, Dickie."

"Yeah, practical jokes," Richard said. "Sending me to the hardware store to get a left-handed monkey wrench. Putting a raw pullet egg dipped in chocolate in my school lunch. I had yolk on my shirt all afternoon. Everybody laughed."

"Nah. I don't remember that, Dickie," Elwood said, biting his lip, stifling a smirk. "I useta ask you if you wanted to go for a ride, and then I'd put you in the back seat while I drove the car from the driveway into the garage. Musta pulled that on you a dozen times."

"At least."

"Same thing with my fart-finger. I could get you to tug at two-three times a week. I always figured you'd catch on, Dickie, but you never did. You was more like your mother when it came to jokes. Anyway, remember when them chain letters used to come to the house? You know, the ones that said you'd die or get some terrible disease if you broke the chain? I always went to the library and got some phone book from Buffalo or Detroit and mailed them letters to names I just picked out of the phone books. See, that was pretty funny, sending chain letters to people you never heard of. You could imagine them gettin' that thing and wonderin' how you knew them. And the good part was, you didn't get your friends mad at you for sending them those stupid letters. I wasn't a superstitious man, Dickie, but at the same time, you don't wanna take unnecessary chances. I mean, I knew a fella once broke a chain letter and his dog got hit by a car, then lightning burned his garage—all in the same week."

Richard grinned. "Yeah, I sort of remember those. You had me mail them out for you once." He chuckled.

"Well, I want this to be the one last little joke, Dickie." Elwood sat at the table and sniffed. "Meat's smellin' pretty good."

"So what's the joke, Dad?"

"When you get my ashes back from the mortuary, just put me in some old shoe box or a Mason jar. Get some of them manila envelopes and some out of town phone books. Put ashes into the envelopes and mail them to folks from the out of town phone books. Send me all over the country, Dickie. It'll be a real kick."

"I can't do that, Dad. It's probably illegal."

"Who'd know? I mean, you don't put no return address on the envelopes. Nobody with any brains would do that. Geez, Dickie, I wouldn'ta thought I'd have to tell you that."

Richard nodded, opened the oven and poked a fork into the roast. "Be a little while yet," he said.

Elwood grunted. "So how was your day, Dickie? I worked like hell on them arborvitae."

"So-so," Richard said. He sat at the kitchen table and rocked back on the chair.

"Don't do that, Dickie. You'll bust the legs on the chair." Elwood sat. "Dickie, I don't want you to laugh, but I done something you probably think is kinda dumb."

Richard thumped forward in the chair, and cast a puzzled glance at his father.

"I made an appointment to see somebody."

"Yeah, who?"

"A doctor, sort of."

"What do you mean, sort of, Dad?"

"That's what I mean, sort of. He calls himself a doctor, but he don't work in a clinic or a hospital."

Richard groaned. "What does he do, Dad?"

"Don't laugh, Dickie. He hypnotizes people and they say he really helps them with their problems."

"Hypnotists are quacks, Dad. Really, I—"

"I told you not to laugh, Dickie."

"I'm not laughing, Dad, I'm sober as a judge, for crying out loud."

"I can't stand it when you laugh at me, Dickie. That superior sort of laugh when you think I'm an idiot. I know the laugh, Dickie."

"I never laughed, Dad. I don't find any of this one bit funny."

Elwood snuffed out his cigarette. "Yeah, well, I know what you're thinkin', Dickie. Always could tell what your mother thought too. Read her like a book."

"Dad, pay attention to what I'm saying. I never laughed. Now start at the beginning and tell me why you want to see this hypnotist. Who is he? Where is his office?"

Elwood cleared his throat. "Dr. Incapace—forgot his first name. He's got this office in the Titan Mall—took that vacant space next to Hoskar Bunting's place. You remember Hoskar, Dickie. Conceptual artist, works in concrete. Hell of a fellow, Hoskar. Good friend of mine too. We'll drop in and visit one of these days. Anyway, Hoskar recommends Dr. Incapace. And so does Emil Slepka. You met him that night at Art's Place. Did him a world of good."

"Dad," Richard said, "a strip mall hypnotist? I've seen that place, and he's got a pink neon sign on the roof. He's a snake-oil guy, Dad. You stay away from him."

"Says I got unresolved issues in my life, Dickie. Says a person needs to exercise them issues. What do you suppose he means by that, Dickie? How do you exercise issues?"

"Geez, Dad." Richard groaned. "ExORcise, not exERcise. It means to get rid of them."

"Why didn't he say so? I had no idea what this bird was talkin' about, and I was wonderin' what in hell Hoskar and Emil saw in him." Elwood drained his beer. "'Course now it makes perfect sense. You don't wanna have unresolved issues cluttering up your life. That's how he put it, and I don't, Dickie."

"You don't need a strip mall quack to resolve your issues, Dad. You could talk to your friends and save yourself a lot of money and worry. You don't need to see this guy anymore."

Elwood dragged on his cigarette and held the smoke in his lungs for several seconds before exhaling an explosive stream. "Got another appointment tonight at 7:30," he said. "I better keep it."

❖❖❖❖❖

The Titan Mall was tucked just inside the Cloquet city limits, and was home to—in addition to the hypnotist and Hoskar Bunting—a dry cleaners, a small restaurant called EAT, a boarded-up filling station, The Trophy Case, Pete's Shoe Repair, Mimsy's

Live Bait, and The Carlton County Shoppers' Guide—Custom Printing.

On the 15-minute drive from home to mall hypnotist, road construction detoured them through town, past the service station on the corner of Highways 45 and 33 that had been designed years ago by the architect Frank Lloyd Wright. "That there's the only time ol' whatisname ever designed a gas station, Dickie," Elwood said, pointing. "Sort of looks like it wants to up and fly away, don't it?"

"Frank Lloyd Wright designed it," Richard said. "How could anyone forget?"

"Who needs a gas station to look fancy?" Elwood said. "What's the point? I mean, who climbs two flights of stairs to look out the window of some old gas station? I could see it maybe if you had a better view of the St. Louie River, or stuff was going on, you know? I never understood why a fella would spend all that money for just a gas station."

Richard shrugged. "Gives folks something to talk about, anyway."

"Not anymore, it don't. When they built it, people gabbed, but not now. Years ago folks drove up from Duluth just to get a fill, but what sense does that make? I mean gasoline is just gasoline."

After a few moments of silence, Richard attempted again to convince Elwood he didn't need a hypnotist—he didn't need anything except maybe a couple aspirins. Elwood remained adamant, however, and when he parked the Checker, told Richard he could either join him in the doctor's office, wait in the car, or get himself a cup of coffee at EAT. Richard said he was going inside.

In the middle of Dr. Tomaso Incapace's waiting room were three concrete foundation blocks arranged in a T. Crumbling chards of concrete lay haphazardly near the blocks. Elwood gave the blocks a cursory look, picked up a two year-old issue of *Opera News* and sat in a chair.

Richard sat next to him and pointed at the blocks. "What's that?"

Elwood lowered his magazine. "Why, that's art, son. Hoskar Bunting gave it to the doc. He's just startin' out and couldn't afford no original art, so Hoskar up and made this for him."

Richard looked at his father. "This isn't art, Dad." He chuckled. "It's three bricks in the middle of a room, and it's crumbling all over the carpet."

"Y'know, Dickie, it never ceases to amaze me how little you know for a fella with all that education. Old Hoskar's a conceptual artist, but he's taken it to a new level. Do I haveta explain

Indians In The Arborvitae

everything? What you got here, Dickie-bird is conceptual art, which is a style designed to reflect the idea of the creator of a work. Old Hoskar's accented content while neglecting form. Ya might say he utilized the eccentric and disposable materials to create awareness of an event or idea. All this stuff evolved from minimal art and whatchamacallit—happenings.

'We got this innovator practically in our neighborhood, creating some of the most astonishing work in contemporary art today, and all you can say is it's three bricks." Elwood shook his head. "I suppose the next thing you're gonna tell me is that you could do that yourself."

"That's right. I could. And so could you—or practically anybody for that matter."

Another patient lowered her copy of *Architectural Digest*. "I sympathize with you, sir," she said to Elwood. "I take it this man is your son." She scowled at Richard and removed her glasses. "What's the matter with young people today? They've turned stodgy, intractable and inflexible. Young man, you clearly fail to see or appreciate that art is an unending process of creation." She smiled and stood. "Now what do you suppose the artist had in mind when he made this arrangement?" She looked at Richard.

"I wouldn't hazard a guess."

"Go ahead," encouraged the woman. "Be wild and free. Hazard, young man."

Richard studied the concrete arrangement again. "To be honest, it looks like a worker has left these blocks here while he took a break. Or maybe he left them this way overnight."

The woman beamed. "Well, well," she said, nodding at Elwood. "Did you tell him what this piece is titled?"

Elwood shook his head. "Never noticed no title myself."

"Coffee break," the woman said. "This work is titled Coffee Break."

"I'll be damned," said Elwood. "Makes sense though, don't it?"

Richard groaned. "Dad, it's junk. This isn't art. It isn't sculpture. It's three concrete blocks. How can you get so easily snookered?"

The woman frowned. "It's the process you must come to appreciate, young man. Process is all."

Just then a beaming Dr. Incapace stepped into the waiting room. "Ah, Elwood Fundy. Nice to see you." He sized Richard. "Are you waiting for an appointment, sir?"

Richard shook his head. "I'm here with my father." He indicated Elwood.

"You're worried about your dad," Dr. Incapace said. "He's really in pretty good shape. But there are these unresolved issues.

No need to go into those. I suspect you know all about them. Nice to meet you." He looked at Elwood. "Well, come on, Elwood, let's get started."

As Richard started to stand, Elwood forced him back into the chair. "Uh-uh, Dickie. This is between me and the doctor. You wait here. Behave yourself and we'll get an ice cream cone on the way home." He chuckled, as did the woman and Dr. Incapace, who led Elwood into a counseling room and closed the door.

The woman picked up a sketch pad and began drawing. Richard leafed through an ancient issue of *Loving Yourself*, occasionally glancing toward Dr. Incapace's counseling room.

Forty-five minutes after entering the hypnotist's office, Elwood returned to the waiting room, wan and shrunken.

Richard sprang to his feet. "Dad, are you all right?"

Elwood reached for his son's arm with trembling fingers. "Let's just go home, Dickie," he said.

Chapter Five

Richard drove the Checker home with Elwood reclining in the back seat, an occasional moan escaping his lips. He did not respond to Richard's questions about what was wrong, what had happened in the hypnotist's office.

Richard parked the car in the driveway next to his minivan and assisted his father out of the back seat. "Dad, I don't like this one bit," he said.

"Me neither, Dickie," Elwood said. "Got to resolve the issues—one of 'em anyway." Elwood leaned heavily on Richard as they made their way to the house.

"What issues, Dad? I mean, the arborvitae are gone, so that's one big issue you don't have to think about."

"Arborvitae was just a symptom, Dickie. Goes a lot deeper than that."

"What does, Dad?"

Elwood sighed. "I think I'll just go up to bed. That session took the wind out of my sails."

"Dad, you've got to forget about this hypnotist nonsense. The guy's a phony, and no good can come of this. Look how upset he's made you. You turned into an old man in less than an hour."

"I got to bear my burdens, Dickie. Same as you. I got stuff to think about, same as you."

"Of course you do, Dad. Nobody says you don't. But you certainly don't need some strip mall shyster taking money from you and making you miserable in the process. Your basic nature is as a fun-loving guy, Dad. It's enough that one of us is morose. But both of us? If that's the case we may not be able to live in the same house together."

"Yeah. I know," Elwood started a slow ascent on the stairs to his bedroom.

Before classes the next morning, Richard stopped by the principal's office hoping to speak to him. But Dr. Piquete wasn't in yet. He hadn't returned from the Rotary Club breakfast. Richard asked Dorothy to take a message—it was imperative he speak with Dr. Piquete before the end of the day. He remained in the office to empty his mail slot when he was tapped on the shoulder. He turned around to face a beaming Marvella Grace, the school's legendary vocal music instructor. As a youngster, she reportedly had studied in New York with Metropolitan Opera coloratura, Amelita Galli-Curci.

As he was about to greet her, Miss Grace warbled, "Go-ood Morrrning, Mr. Fundy. I've learned all about you," she continued, smiling warmly. She adjusted a bobby pin in the French roll of her ash-blond hair. "You came to us from Blessed Assurance Life and Casualty. They've certainly taken excellent care of me for all the 45 years I've taught at Button Gwinnet. You just can't beat them. I haven't needed to submit even one claim. What do you think of that?" She laughed. "My how time does fly."

"Yes," Richard said, "it does."

Miss Grace put her fleshy, liver-spotted hand on Richard's elbow, and led him away from the mail slots. She leaned toward him and in a conspiratorial whisper said she understood he was feeling blue.

"I'm fine, Miss Grace, really."

"That's not what Hilda tells me. She and I have been great friends for many, many years, young man."

"I have a class in a few minutes, Miss Grace, and I—"

"It's succor, isn't it? And don't I know exactly what you mean, young man. Well, maybe not quite exactly, but I have some experience with people who suffer a heartsickness such as yours."

She paused for a deep breath. "I've never breathed a word of this to anyone else, and I trust what I'm about to say won't leave here."

"Can this wait? I really have to get to my room."

Miss Grace put her hand on his arm and squeezed. "I know, but there is hope for you. My nephew was for many years a troubled young man. Raised on the family farm, where my brother grew radishes, but the boy was oh, so troubled. He wasn't succored, you see. Well, I urged him to get help for himself, though I had no idea what his issues were. And I won't prod you for your particulars either. But not long after Ethan—that's my nephew—joined a support group for transgender radish growers like himself, it just saved his life."

Richard blinked. "Uh, that's not my problem, Miss Grace." He backed toward the door.

"I don't mean to infer that it is. But each of us needs succoring. You're in desperate need of music, Mr. Fundy," she said brightly. She clutched both his hands in hers. "Find time for music, plumb the depths of your soul. Something as simple as music may be all the comforting you require at this time. Do you read me, Mr. Fundy? Music has the capacity to reach the very core of your being. I'd be pleased to lend you recordings and tapes of splendid, soaring, majestic arias and symphonies. Hours and hours worth. They will infuse you with their healing balm." She smiled again. "We can't have one of our new faculty looking like a basset hound, can we? We cannot. Music is transporting, and it will transport you, Mr. Fundy."

"Thank you, yes. I appreciate your concern, Miss Grace, but as it is one minute until the bell rings, I must transport myself to class." He offered a perfunctory nod, and moved away, stepping around two teachers talking in the office doorway. As he walked rapidly down the hall, he heard Miss Grace call, "Embrace the music, Mr. Fundy. And plumb the depths of your soul."

After dismissing his last hour class, Richard headed for the office and bumped into Adrian LaGrande. "Hey, sport," Adrian said, "everything okay? I mean this business with Hilda."

"Fine, Adrian. Everything's just hunky-dory."

"Geez, I hope so. Our Miss Grace was at my table during lunch and said she'd talked to you." Adrian smiled. "Same old same old with that gal. 'Plumb the depths of your soul,' and all that crap. I'll bet she laid that on you too, right?"

Richard chuckled. "As a matter of fact, she did."

"You better tell her you plumbed the depths, Rich. She'll be on you like a dog on a bone until you say you sought solace in longhair music." Adrian laughed. "Well, have a good night, sport." He waved and started down the hall in the opposite direction.

Richard turned in to the office. "He's expecting you, Mr. Fundy," Dorothy said, looking up from her desk and smiling sweetly.

"Thanks." Richard stepped past her and knocked on the principal's closed door.

Dr. Piquete opened the door. "Ah, Fundy, Fundy. *Entrez-vous, s'il vous plait.*" He stood back and indicated a chair opposite his desk for Richard. Dr. Piquete was again in red stocking feet.

"Dr. Piquete, I must come clean immediately about Button Gwinnet and put an end to the charade that's starting to insinuate itself into our community."

Dr. Piquete wiped his glasses with his handkerchief. His smile dissolved as he looked at Richard. "Whatever are you talking about, Fundy?"

Richard inhaled, then exhaled audibly through pursed lips. "Just this—Gwinnet was essentially a zero, Dr. Piquete. Maybe we should simply call ourselves Brackett Senior High School. Besides, it seems to me that our citizens would prefer that."

The principal slammed a book on his desktop. "Now hold on a minute, Fundy. Not you too. This revisionist garbage has gone too far, and I'd have thought you'd be above that sort of thing—that you wouldn't be flamboozled by polemical, errant scholarship. And people can call this school what they will, but our official name is Button Gwinnet, and so long as I am principal, it is how we will be referred to."

Richard blew a long exhalation before speaking. "The plain fact is, Dr. Piquete, our Button Gwinnet was no paragon. To be blunt, sir, he was an accident at best, who happened to be in the right place at the right time. There's really precious little to commend him for. In fact, if it were up to me, I'd try to get the school renamed."

"Damn!" cried Dr. Piquete, banging his fist on the desktop, knocking a small lamp on the floor, where it broke. "Damn again!" He did not move to pick up the pieces.

Sighing, Richard leaned down and gathered several shards and dumped them in the wastebasket.

"Oh leave that be, Fundy, for heaven's sake. Who gives a diddly-toot about a cheap lamp at a time like this? I don't think you perceive the gravity of your statement. Are you absolutely certain of this?"

Richard nodded. "I'm afraid I am. There's just no getting around it."

The principal stood and strode to the window overlooking the football field below. "Yes," he said, not facing Richard. "Yes, there are ways around it. And you, Fundy, must find one of those circumventions. There's the pride of our institution, the pride of our community at stake here."

"I'm aware of that. But on the other hand—"

"I won't hear of it, Fundy," the principal erupted, clapping his hands over his ears. "Not for a minute. Consider this, sir— generations of pupils march across the stage each spring to receive diplomas. You should see their faces beaming with pride, the love radiating from the eyes of parents and relatives. It's a sight to behold, Fundy. And why is that? It's because these young people have given four years of their lives to this institution. They proudly wear letter jackets. They continue to carry the name of Button Gwinnet throughout their lives, wherever whimsy takes them—to hospitals, battleships, as bellhops and doctors, as millwrights and farriers. Wherever there are good citizens striving for a better life, for a better world, there are graduates of Button Gwinnet Senior High School at the forefront, waiting to be counted. And Fundy, I simply won't allow you to spoil all that with a casual snapping of the fingers." Dr. Piquete attempted to snap his own fingers for effect, producing a barely audible click.

Richard groaned softly and felt perspiration slide beneath his glasses. "It would be imprudent to deceive, Dr. Piquete."

Hulot Piquete whirled about and shook his finger at Richard. "Speak not of deception, Fundy, which is a grave, grave offense. You begin with this very signal accomplishment of Mr. Gwinnet. He was indisputably a signer of the Declaration, was he not?'

"Yes, of course he was."

Dr. Piquete smiled. "Well, how many people can say they signed the Declaration of Independence? A measly handful. And Gwinnet was one of them. Let's not ever forget that. So..." Dr. Piquete clasped his hands behind him and stepped around his desk, striding toward Richard, then executed an about-face and paused again before the window. He released his hands and faced Richard. "Emphasize that, Fundy, and its importance to history, and subsequently, to all of us. I know you can bring it off," he said, his faint smile dissolving. "You must bring it off. Need I emphasize that a little ingratiating on the part of a non-tenured teacher would not be out of line? Indeed, I think I needn't." He smiled again. "You're excused, Fundy," he said, turning back to the window.

"Dr. Piquete, really," said Richard, rising. "Wouldn't it be better if—"

"It most certainly would not," the principal said, not looking at Richard. "Most certainly not. As CEO of this institution, I have many to answer to, and abrogating pride in my school would assuredly cut against the quick, Fundy." He faced the teacher. "You have your assignment, and I expect you'll carry it out." He gave a dismissive wave of his hand. "There's not that much time until the Sanguine Society luncheon, and the fellows have every right to anticipate a crackerjack performance from you."

Richard started for the door, then turned around. He was about to say he wouldn't, he *couldn't* make a speech to the Sanguine Society, but Dr. Piquete quickly bolted past him, exiting his office, and hurrying down the hall.

Richard picked up his brief case and left for home.

Elwood had fallen asleep in front of the television set. Two cigarettes, burned to the filter, were in the ashtray. His lips were pulled down at the corners, and his breathing was interspersed with low, aspirate moans. Richard tiptoed past him, but Elwood startled him. "Dickie," he stated.

Richard turned around, but Elwood's eyes remained closed. Richard continued into the kitchen. "Dickie, I'm talking to you," Elwood called.

Richard placed his briefcase on the kitchen table and returned to the living room. "I thought you were napping, Dad."

"Was, but not no more. I never been one to talk in my sleep, Dickie. You know me better'n that." He still had not opened his eyes.

"You sure you're not still sleeping? Your eyes are closed, Dad."

"You tryin' to be funny or what, Dickie? 'Course I'm awake. My eyes are tired from TV, I guess." Elwood opened his eyes and rubbed them. He leaned forward and snapped off the television with the remote control. "I was dreamin' about exORcisin' them unresolved issues. Thing is when you're sleepin' and dreamin', you just go ahead and get yourself resolved. But as you know, Dickie, real life ain't that way. A fella can be unresolved for years."

Richard sat on the sofa across from his father. "What ought to be resolved here and now, Dad, is your decision to stop seeing that quack. That guy's gonna bleed you dry if you're not careful. I'm going to make some calls and find out if this guy's legit, and if he's not—"

"He's helping me, Dickie. Don't that mean nothin' to you?"

Richard sighed. "Dad, I just don't want to see you taken advantage of, that's all."

Elwood stood. "Ain't gonna ever happen again, Dickie. It's maybe happened before, but sure as shootin' ain't gonna happen again. Once a man gets his peace of mind back, he's not likely to want to give it up." He drummed his fists against his thighs. Richard sighed again and smoothed his eyebrows.

"Take me for a ride, Dickie," Elwood said suddenly. He scooped a light jacket from behind the recliner and started putting it on.

"Now? I've got papers to look at and dinner to get started. We can take a drive after supper if you want."

"Now, Dickie," Elwood said, moving toward the door. "I don't feel like driving, so you get the job. I'll be in the car."

Richard banged his fist on the arm of the chair, and his father whirled about. "That's not nice, Dickie," Elwood said, frowning. "Sorta like back-talk when you was a kid. I think after all I been through, that I'm entitled to a little respect from you. I can't whip you no more, Dickie, but it seems to me there are lessons you never learned, and being as you're practically middle-aged, you won't ever learn 'em."

"Okay, Dad," Richard said, standing, his palms outstretched. "You win."

"I usually do, Dickie. In the end I usually do win." He cleared his throat. "Dickie, you ever think of gettin' remarried? I know what I said at the church about you not bein' the remarrying type, but shoot, a fella can change. Look at me. Anyway, I got to thinkin' about your marrying again. Lucy whatsername?—that girl you used to date in high school—Parlotear. Her first marriage flopped too, but you know what, Dickie? She come back to Cloquet and started up a business, a whaddaya callit—fitness center. Got all these fat old babes come in two-three times a week, jumpin' up and down, sweatin' like stuck pigs, and payin' fifty bucks a month to Lucy. So what I'm sayin', Dickie, is you should try to cozy up to her. She useta be kinda sweet on you, it seemed to me. And you wouldn't be a half-bad husband to her if you put your mind to it. I'd like to see you settled before I die, Dickie. It would have meant a lot to your mother, who made me promise I'd take care of you." Elwood shrugged. "I done my best; no one can say I didn't. You call Lucy, Dickie."

"Dad—I heard she's about to be married again quite soon."

"So? She ain't married yet, Dickie. And she's rollin' in the do-re-mi. You'd have something to fall back on after you lose this teaching job."

"What makes you think I'll lose my job, Dad?"

"Oh, you're probably a good enough teacher, Dickie, but it's just this feelin' I got." He coughed. "Think about it. Now time's wastin'. Let's vamoose."

From the Checker's back seat, Elwood directed Richard to drive

Indians In The Arborvitae

toward Cloquet, and across the St. Louis River, down through Scanlon, up 14th Street to Baldridge Avenue and, turning right on County Road 115, they drove toward Squaw Creek.

"Driver, pull over right here," Elwood ordered, and Richard braked the car.

"Okay, whatever you say, Dad."

"Lookie there, Dickie. A tree fulla Fireside apples. My all-time favorite."

Richard grinned. "Yeah. They're very good."

Elwood got out of the car and stretched. "I'd like one right now. How about you, Dickie?"

"Maybe a bit later, after supper. We can stop at the market on our way home."

"No, Dickie. I want some of these." He pointed to the back yard tree situated about 40 feet from a two-story yellow house.

Richard paled and forced a laugh. "You know these folks?"

Elwood shook his head. "I don't have no idea who these birds are, Dickie." He started walking toward the yard.

"Hold on, Dad," Richard called, scrambling out from behind the wheel. "You're not thinking of stealing apples, are you?" He forced another chortle.

"Look, a bunch already fell on the ground. These folks can't use all them apples." He continued walking, calling back over his shoulder. "You climb the tree and give her a little shake and I'll grab three-four nice ones. We'll share, Dickie. Even-Steven."

Richard grabbed his father's arm. "Dad, let's be serious for a minute, okay? We aren't even going to think about stealing apples."

"All right, Dickie. We'll borrow a few that nobody will miss."

"Dad."

Elwood pulled away from Richard, pushed through a lilac hedge, and emerged into the yard, where he walked toward the tree. He paused and looked around. "If you ain't gonna help me, Dickie, at least keep your eyes open for you-know-who." Elwood spit on his hands, grabbed a low branch and attempted to swing himself into the first crotch on the apple tree. He slid back to the ground. He repeated the process with the same result. He glanced around before calling his son. "There's no one home, Dickie. Now come and give me a hand."

Richard entered the yard and tried to pull his father away. "Dad, this has gone far enough."

Elwood withdrew roughly, and tried climbing once more. This time Richard gave him a boost. "That's more like it, Dickie," Elwood rasped, slightly out of breath. "Now, I'm gonna shake that big branch yonder, and you pick up the apples, then help me down."

Richard stood aside, hands in his pockets. Elwood cautiously crept up a couple feet onto the first large branch. He held on with both hands. "I could break my neck, Dickie."

Richard nodded. "Indeed."

Elwood made a feeble attempt to sway the branch. One apple fell. "Grab it, Dickie," he whispered hoarsely. "She's got my name all over it."

Richard did not move until an officer entered the yard, pausing, glancing from Elwood to Richard, then removing his cap and scratching his head. "What is this? What do you fellas think you're doing, anyway?"

Elwood forced a laugh. "The boy here is afraid of heights," he said. "I'm getting' old for this, but hey, whaddaya gonna do when you get hungry for apples?"

"Dad." Flushing, Richard stepped toward the officer.

"Whaddaya think you're doin' up there?" The officer ran a hand through his hair. Then he approached the tree and extended a hand to Elwood, aiding the older man's descent.

Elwood dusted his hands on his pants. "Thank you, sir. You gotta tell Dickie here everything. You didn't see him come help his father down, did you? He'da done it, but you'd hafta say something first. You just up and done it, and I appreciate it. Now I'd like your name and badge number so I can write a nice letter to your supervisor about you. A letter of commendation, I think they call it. I'll get on that right away." Elwood nodded for emphasis.

The officer looked at Richard, then back at Elwood. He shook his head. "Do you know whose place this is?"

Richard, pale, groaned. Elwood grinned. "Sure. Fella with a real nice Fireside tree in the yard. Just about the best local apple there is for my money."

"Dammit, this is my yard, my tree, and just what in hell do you think you're doing here?" The officer passed his hat from hand to hand.

Elwood cleared his throat and spit. "Tell him, Dickie," he said.

The squat, muscular officer turned toward Richard and approached him, drawing close enough so Richard was able to see his name plate—Deputy Sheriff Whitsung. There was a perspiration line around the collar of his light blue short-sleeved shirt. "Well?" He squared off before Richard, who stepped back two paces.

"Umm," Richard said.

"Just tell him, Dickie," coached Elwood, leaning against the Fireside trunk. He surreptitiously reached down and plucked an apple from the ground and put it in his jacket pocket. "Tell him so we can get home for dinner."

"You know, I could run you fellas in for something like this," Deputy Whitsung said, advancing another step toward Richard. "But I feel kinda sorry for the old guy, and hells bells, I got enough to take care of without running in a couple old fart adults for cooning apples."

"We're terribly sorry, officer, and I can assure you it won't happen again." Richard shook his head. "I—"

"You count on it not happening no more," the deputy said, nodding. "Now, let me see some identification."

"I don't have nothin' with me, but Dickie does," Elwood said.

Richard produced his wallet and handed it to the officer, who carefully examined it, removing several cards and slips of paper. He studied one for several seconds, then, shaking his head, looked up at Richard. "You a school teacher at Brackett Senior? A damn school teacher stealing apples. This is a kid's game, mister. What the hell were you thinking?"

Elwood, lighting a cigarette and exhaling through his nostrils, stepped forward. "Now hold on, officer. This whole thing was my fault. Dickie was only doing what his daddy told him to do. It was me who wanted the apples, not Dickie. Shoot, take me to jail if you must, but leave the boy out of this."

The officer turned from Elwood to Richard. "Well if that doesn't beat all. You ought to be ashamed of yourself, letting this old fellow take the fall for you." He returned Richard's wallet. "I'm gonna try to forget this ever happened. But don't *you* ever forget it." He shook his index finger at Richard. "And I'm gonna say this just once—anybody complains about their apple trees bein' raided, I come lookin' for you, and I won't go so easy on you next time. And one other thing, if the school board goes around hiring teachers like you, Mr. Fundy, I sure as hell won't be voting for no more school tax increases, and I'll work like a dog to see every one of them goes straight down the tubes. Now get the hell off my property. The sight of you makes me wanna throw up."

He watched as Richard and Elwood pushed through the lilac shrubs and got into the Checker. Richard slowly pulled away from the curb and headed down the street, coming to a full stop at the intersection before turning left. His fingers, tense on the wheel, whitened.

Elwood, from the back seat, cleared his throat. "If you'd have just done like I said, Dickie—got up and shook the tree—we'da been long gone before that officer come home and seen us. You can't expect a man my age with my agility to take on a project like that. That's the responsibility of younger fellas. Shoot, we'd have been long gone down the road before you could say Jack Robinson." He extracted an apple from his pocket. "Got one, anyway, Dickie," he said, taking a large bite. "Umm—good."

Chapter Six

Richard drove home. He did not speak when Elwood asked about dinner. The Fireside apple, Elwood said, would never take the place of a regular meal, though maybe if he'd gotten two or three of them he might forget about supper.

Richard went straight to his room and didn't leave it all night, except to use the bathroom. Elwood did not mention dinner again, and Richard wasn't certain if his father opened cans or made sandwiches, or indeed, whether he ate anything.

Richard lay fully clothed atop his bed pondering the apple tree experience, and trying to fashion positive material about Button Gwinnet. But his thoughts seemed incoherent, so he gave up entirely, undressed, and retired at nine p.m.

He woke shortly before five, tiptoed into the bathroom for morning ablutions, then crept downstairs for a breakfast of corn flakes, grape juice, instant coffee and a somewhat stale supermarket danish. He was backing his van out of the driveway before six and heading to school.

The radio was tuned to a popular early morning drive-time program that marginally engaged Richard until he heard a listener talking about area schools, how unmentionable bodily functions were discussed in classes, as if that were important to education, and was it any wonder that kids graduating from high school these days can't spell their names, and now he heard that quite recently one of the district's high school teachers had been caught stealing apples out of a local citizen's back yard tree. "Is it any wonder kids turn out the way they are?" the listener harangued. "A teacher like that should be fired, no questions asked."

The program host agreed, and said he found it hard to

believe such a thing, but in this day and age (one could almost see him shaking his head before the microphone) you can't discount anything. "Teachers are only human," he said in a mocking tone. "No different from you or I. Hey, be right back after this break."

His pulse quickening in his throat, Richard snapped off the radio and continued to school, where the entire front row of the parking lot was vacant, save the Chevy pick-up pride and joy of Carlyle Justen, the head custodian. He pulled up next to it, grabbed his papers and books and entered the building. Carlyle was standing in the entry smoking a cigarette, despite the rules against smoking except in the basement boiler room.

Carlyle was holding a small transistor radio in his hand, listening to the talk show that Richard had turned off in his car. "Been listening to Chauncey Booth this morning?" he said, flicking his live cigarette out onto the front sidewalk. Richard grunted. "One of the teachers apparently got busted swiping apples right here in town. Idiot. I mean what could that joker been thinking? Y'know, wouldn't halfway surprise me if it was Adrian. There's just something about that guy." Carlyle shook his head. "Always stuck me as an odd bird, know what I mean?" He looked at Richard. "Sorry. Maybe I shouldn't of said nothing. You and him are sorta tight, I understand."

"I'm sure it wasn't Adrian, Carlyle. Anyway, the whole thing could be a rumor."

Carlyle shrugged. "Well, if it ain't a rumor, I wouldn't put it past Adrian. Guys with funny names sometimes do funny things. Ya never know."

Richard nodded, moving quickly beyond Carlyle toward his room at the end of the hall. The custodian stayed with him. "What makes some people tick?" he said. "Don't ya just wonder? A teacher pulled crap like that in my day, his ass is grass, know what I mean?"

"Yeah," Richard acknowledged quietly. "Got a ton of papers to look at," he added, not facing Carlyle, then walked briskly to his classroom.

He snapped on the lights and tossed his coat over the back of his desk chair and sat. He surprised himself by not immediately concentrating on the ignominy of yesterday, nor of his assignment to resurrect positive history about Button Gwinnet. Instead he was remembering Lucy Parlotear, the girl voted most talkative by his graduating class.

He had dated her two or three times during their senior year, and what he mostly remembered from those dates was Lucy's nonstop prattle. And back then Lucy was rather chunky. Still, there was something to be said for her chatter. You knew she was around and attempted to engage you. Claudia, Richard was thinking, rarely spoke to him during the last two years of their marriage. She was thin, though, ran marathons. And now Lucy was back home, getting remarried. Richard chuckled to himself, thinking perhaps the marriage might succeed if Lucy's new fiancé were hearing impaired.

Then Richard recalled the tender note Lucy had sent following his mother's death, and felt ashamed for his previous thought. He didn't dwell on it because Hilda Narr poking her large head into his room interrupted him. "My but you're early this morning, Mr. Fundy," she said brightly.

"Yes," he said, reaching across his desk to snap on the radio to classical music. "I come in early every once in a while to plumb the depths of my soul, in a manner of speaking."

"Well good for you, Mr. Fundy," she said, gesturing with her fist. "I don't suppose you heard the story about one of ours—possibly one of ours anyway—who was caught stealing apples last night?"

Pretending to shuffle through some papers on his desk, Richard didn't look at Hilda. "I've heard," he said quietly. "Hilda, would you mind if I excused myself this morning. I've got a ton to take care of before first hour class."

"Not a problem, Mr. Fundy. Not at all. I'm encouraged to see you taking care of yourself. We'll talk again." She backed out of the door and offered a small wave before plodding down the hall toward Adrian's room.

Richard removed his Button Gwinnet notes from a large envelope and placed them before him. They proved useless to his assignment. He snapped a pencil in half and tossed both pieces into the wastebasket.

Nearly an hour later, at seven a.m., he had filled several sheets from a yellow legal pad with notes for the Gwinnet presentation. He put the notes in his top desk drawer and glanced at his lesson plan for the day. Students were beginning to meander through the hallway now, and he overheard one of them talking about the teacher who swiped apples.

"You ready, Fundy?" Hulot Piquete marched toward Richard's desk, an anxious smile playing over his lips.

Richard sighed. "I can give it a shot, I guess."

Students careened into the auditorium, jostling, punching, goosing, laughing, causing Hulot Piquete to rap his gavel on the lectern. The sound reverberated into the highly amplified microphone, and secured the desired result. "Students, may I remind you that we have guests today—many of whom are your own parents. Now enough shenanigans. Please take your seats." He glanced over his shoulder at Richard, standing behind him.

As the auditorium quieted, the principal began to speak, introducing Richard as a new member of the Button Gwinnet family this year, an outstanding teacher of American Studies, who had agreed to enlighten the entire community about the school's namesake, about whom, sadly, the community knew little. "But our own Mr. Fundy, a scholar with both a keen and probing intellect, is here to present the story of the man for whom our school is named. Please join me in welcoming Mr. Richard Fundy."

An overly boisterous greeting met Richard's approach to the lectern, and did not quiet until Dr. Piquete again stepped forward and banged the gavel. "Faculty," he announced, gesturing with extended index finger, "I'm requesting you take charge here, and write up any pupil behaving in a fractious manner. If necessary, have those students evicted and sent to the office. We have a golden opportunity this morning to learn something very important, and any disruptions are entirely out of order." He nodded to Richard who stepped forward again and took a drink from the water glass on the stand next to the lectern. He spread his notes before him, including sections from a speech given in 1858 by Abraham Lincoln. He briefly looked out at the students and guests then scanned his notes for the opening statement, momentarily panicking when he failed to locate it. He bore on. "Thank you, Dr. Piquete for your kind introduction." He swallowed, then rambled a while about his first brush with Gwinnet during his junior year at Babiole College.

"But that was a long time ago," Richard said. "And I'd almost forgotten it until Dr. Piquete asked me to give this talk. Button Gwinnet is indeed an unusual name for a man who participated in one of this country's most important events—the signing of the Declaration of Independence. He was in agreement with Thomas Jefferson, who drafted the Declaration, fully supporting the phrase, 'We hold these truths to be self-evident, that all men are created equal; that they are endowed by their creator with certain unalienable rights, that among these are Life, Liberty and the pursuit of Happiness.' To be sure there were more famous signers of the Declaration, including Jefferson himself, Benjamin Franklin, John Adams, and John Hancock.

"And then there were others like Richard Henry Lee of Virginia, Charles Thomson, Thomas Stone, or William Floyd. And of course, Button Gwinnet. These are names quite unfamiliar to most Americans, yet their signatures are on the bottom of what is arguably the most important document in our nation's history. And if we dare not disparage the memory of those men, we also are called to esteem the name of Button Gwinnet, whose history is a

Indians In The Arborvitae

bit murkier than most.

"There are no monuments to him. We don't know for certain where he's buried. We can't visit his home in Georgia, because we don't know the one that may have belonged to him—if indeed it still stands. How unlike this is from say, Charles Carroll, who was the longest living signer when he died in 1832 at the age of 95. The town of Carrollton in Maryland is named for him, and one can visit his house there today near Baltimore. It is open to the public, and is located at 800 East Lombard Street, on the northeast corner of Front and Lombard Streets."

Richard paused, lifting his arms like wings to circulate air into his saturated armpits. Peripherally, he noticed the stiff smile on the face of his principal.

"Then there's the story of Samuel Huntington from Connecticut. He was born in Windham County, Scotland before immigrating to America. But even the Scots have recognized Huntington's importance, and are seeking to restore his boyhood home. Nearly a million dollars is needed for this undertaking, and I have little doubt it will be successful. But can the same be said for Mr. Gwinnet? Sadly, it cannot.

"Button Gwinnet was born in Gloucestershire, England, in 1735, the son of an Anglican vicar. Here in America, the Anglicans are known as Episcopalians. In 1759, the same year he married a grocer's daughter, he entered the export shipping business, and started trading with the colonies. So far so good. Then, we don't exactly know when, he immigrated to Savannah, Georgia. He purchased a store there, but soon sold it and borrowed money to buy St. Catherine's Island off the port of Sunbury. Though deep in debt, he continued borrowing money as poachers and the British navy raided his island and made off with his livestock. Finally creditors took his properties, leaving only the house in his name.

"Despite these adversities, Gwinnet bore on and was elected to the Colonial Assembly in 1769, serving one two-year term. It was during this period that he signed the Declaration of Independence, and earned his mark in history."

Richard coughed and took a sip of water. "After the signing, things went pretty much downhill for Mr. Gwinnet. He applied for commission as a colonel in George Washington's army, but was turned down. He later engaged in a duel with an old rival, and both men were injured. But Gwinnet's wounds developed gangrene and he died a few days later."

"Now there may be those who maintain that Gwinnet was an accident of history, that he was an ordinary man who happened to be a signer of the Declaration of Independence. But these folks would be wrong. Yes, he was an ordinary man who knew many disappointments. But the lesson for all of us is clear. Your life is not measured by your failures, but by how you respond to them. Will you young people, like Button Gwinnet, rise from the ash heap of failure, dust yourselves off and go on to great achievement? This is certainly the destiny a man such as Button Gwinnet would have in mind for us as we hearken to his often pitiful existence, yet at the same time, heroic stance in the face of adversity."

Richard exhaled audibly and arranged Lincoln notes before him. Quoting, but not acknowledging the president, he said, "'I am filled with deep emotion at finding myself standing here, in this place... I have never had a feeling that did not spring from the sentiments embodied in the Declaration of Independence. I have often pondered over the dangers which were incurred by the men who framed and adopted that Declaration of Independence. I have pondered over the toils that were endured by the officers and soldiers of the army who achieved that Independence. I have often inquired of myself what great principle or idea it was that kept this Confederacy so long together. It was not the mere matter of the separation of the Colonies from the motherland; but that sentiment in the Declaration of Independence which gave liberty, not alone to the people of this country, but, I hope, to the world, for all future time. It was that which gave promise that in due time the weight would be lifted from the shoulders of all men.'

"This, my friends, is the contribution of Button Gwinnet, a man nearly forgotten. If I may be so bold as to insert my own thoughts on why history has neglected this man, it seems prudent to assume he was modest—the archtypical American, if you will, who sought no limelight for himself, who thought himself no better than others, and who was led by Providence to do his best for his country without fanfare."

He looked up first at a beaming Hulot Piquete, then at the audience, their faces blank and bored, not realizing, it occurred to him, that he was finished. "Thank you very much," he said finally, and received a scattering of applause.

Dr. Piquete was on his feet before the microphone, shaking Richard's hand. "A hearty thank you, Mr. Fundy, for this thoughtful, informative, and moving presentation. Thank you to our guests for your attendance. I will shortly be joining you in the cafeteria for coffee. Students, you are dismissed to your fourth hour classes."

Perspiring freely, Richard exited the auditorium back stage and encountered Adrian. The teacher was grinning. "Sounded good, Rich," he said. "I never knew the half of it, this stuff about Gwinnet. I probably still don't, but you sure sounded good."

Richard nodded and continued down the hall, pausing for a drink at the fountain. Another teacher whose name he couldn't remember clapped him on the shoulder and said, "Nice job. I mean I didn't have a clue before. We probably should be having a unit on this joker in American History classes, don't you think?"

Richard nodded and continued on his way. "Wonderful, young man," trilled Miss Grace. "An edifying presentation. How I envy you your ability to turn a phrase. You were eloquent." She clasped both his hands and beamed. "Absolutely eloquent. Well, I look forward to seeing you after school today."

"What's after school today?"

"Why, the announcement was in everyone's box, Mr. Fundy." A broad smile creased Miss Grace's face. "It's our faculty sing-out. It's a tradition here. More or less my idea, but heartily endorsed by Dr. Piquete, who's a very solid tenor himself. Yes, it's helped foster closeness within our little Button Gwinnet family. I'm sure you'll find the session edifying. And our wonderful cooks always provide shortbread and coffee. There's hot cider for those of us who eschew caffeine. I'm so looking forward to hearing you sing, Mr. Fundy."

Richard eased his hands from her grasp. "Is attendance required? I mean I've been having some issues with my father and—."

"Well, I hate to think that mandating attendance at faculty functions is necessary," interrupted Miss Grace, her smile dissolving. "But any memo from Dr. Piquete I would think might be considered in that light. Though I'm quite certain that all of us thoroughly enjoy ourselves. Singing releases those inner stresses like nothing else. Singing sustaineth the soul, Mr. Fundy." She began Puccini's "O Mio Babbino Caro," her quavering soprano soaring above the din of teenage banter and horseplay in the hall.

Several students paused to stare at Miss Grace, whose hands were clasped at her bosom. Richard pointed at his watch, signaling it was almost time for class, and he hurried away toward his room.

As he neared it, he was hailed by Dr. Piquete. "Fundy, you can't go to your room now. There are people waiting to see you and talk about your little speech. Leave the class."

"I don't think that's a very good idea," Richard said. "They're a rather unsettled bunch, you know, and—"

"No, no, I've arranged everything." The principal approached Richard and clapped him on the shoulder. "Hilda will be along momentarily to escort them to a study hall. We can't let a moment like this slip by. There are parents, movers and shakers from the area, who are waiting for you in the cafeteria, and you can't, you mustn't, disappoint them."

There was no crowd in the cafeteria, but perhaps a dozen or 15 adults sipping coffee from Styrofoam cups and nibbling the dense shortbread prepared by the kitchen staff at the school. Dr. Piquete drew Richard a coffee from the urn, and beaming, handed it to him. "Here's the star of the assembly," he announced. "I'm sure you have lots of questions, and he'd be more than happy to entertain them."

Richard attempted a smile. He raised the coffee to his lips. It scalded his tongue, and he put the cup down. "I'll do my best," he said.

A woman in a purple sweater with large yellow cat earrings raised her hand. "Have you ever been to Georgia, Mr. Fundy? I ask only because the Gwinnet name still carries a certain cachet down there. However, I must say I learned more from your talk than during the two years we lived there while my husband was in the service." She coughed into the crook of her arm, and excused herself. "I used to hear this rumored a little when we lived there, and I wonder if you could comment on it. There was talk that Button Gwinnet was an amoral drunkard ."

"Revisionist rubbish," snapped Dr. Piquete.

"I can't speak to that, ma'am," said Richard. "I've never come across any such information."

"Certainly not." Dr. Piquete nodded assertively.

Richard fielded several other less provocative questions, and Dr. Piquete thanked the adults for coming. Richard poured out his now tepid coffee, and started to leave the cafeteria.

Dr. Piquete joined him. "You might have answered the purple woman's question more aggressively. I don't personally fault your response, but the mere fact that such a question was raised, and you didn't emphatically deny the rumor, why it shouldn't surprise me if, in time, people come to accept it as truth. You know how people are quick to grasp salacious falsehood." The principal was frowning. "But I suppose we'll have to fight that battle when it erupts. On the whole, Fundy, you acquitted yourself well, and this was a nice little tune-up for the speech before the Sanguine Society." The principal continued walking with Richard. He occasionally waved and greeted other faculty and students.

As they reached Richard's classroom, Dr. Piquete touched Richard's elbow. "Say, Fundy, I don't suppose you've heard anything about a district teacher being arrested for stealing apples out of a back yard tree, have you?"

"I know nothing about an...arrest." His jaw tightened.

Dr. Piquete nodded. "Just wondering, of course. I sure hope it wasn't anybody from our staff. Nobody seems to know anything, though Carlyle thinks it might have been Adrian La Grande. Until the man is charged, police won't release his name either." He shook his head. "A thing like this is very bad for the image, Fundy. Could set our credibility back for years." He put his hand on Richard's arm. "Say, I could call Ray Whitsung—he's a Sanguine who's with the sheriff's department. Maybe he knows something about this."

Blanching, Richard started to open his door, offering his profile to the principal as he spoke. "But he couldn't release the name in any case?"

"No, of course not. However, he might be willing to tell me if the perpetrator was at least someone from this faculty." He clapped Richard on the shoulder. "You needn't bother yourself about this. Again, my deepest appreciation for your presentation today. Oh, by the way, if you sing as well as you speak, you'll have proved yourself a wonderful addition to this faculty."

Richard entered Miss Grace's music room, and Dr. Piquete, standing on the top riser, beckoned him up. He nodded at the principal and started to help himself to a Styrofoam cup of coffee from the urn in the front of the room. "Not yet, Fundy," Dr. Piquete called. "You don't want caffeine on your throat before singing. You have time for a quick shortbread, and perhaps a swallow or two of cider, which I highly recommend. Coffee drinkers really ought to wait until we're finished."

Several sour-faced male faculty rolled their eyes at the pronouncement, and Richard exhaled audibly and ignored the shortbread left over from this morning's reception. "You're a tenor, I bet," Dr. Piquete called again, and indicated Richard should stand next to him on the riser.

He climbed up and scanned the room. Adrian LaGrande was not present. Hilda Narr, however, stood with what appeared to be a tenor section. She smiled and moved to make room for Richard between her and Dr. Piquete. "I always help out the men," she said. "Not enough tenors. And the basses hardly ever sing out."

"Hilda is a valuable utility man. She fits in almost anywhere." Dr. Piquete patted her shoulder. "I mean no disrespect when I say Hilda would be able to sing with the bass section too." He smiled.

"Do-re-mi," sang Hilda in a mock basso profundo. She nudged Richard and chortled.

Finally Miss Grace took her place behind a podium and waved her hands above her head for attention. "It's just wonderful to see everybody here again. Let me begin by stating, as I do each and every year when we gather like this, that the faculty that sings together, clings together." Miss Grace beamed and looked fondly at her principal. "Do you have any announcements before we get underway, Dr. Piquete?"

"Wonder where Adrian is?" Dr. Piquete remarked before smiling and raising his voice. "Nothing really, Miss Grace, except to welcome Richard Fundy to our sing-session. And to once more express the appreciation of our entire faculty and community for his excellent presentation this morning on our namesake." He led the faculty in applauding Richard, who flushed slightly, but bobbed his head in acknowledgement.

After thanking Dr. Piquete, Miss Grace announced they'd begin with the school song, which opened with a spoken cheer: "Beat 'em, Button, beat 'em. Beat 'em, Button, beat 'em. Beat 'em, Button, beat 'em, Button, beat 'em, Button, beat 'em." An *a cappella* version of the Washington and Lee march followed. "When e'er the boys from Button fall in line, they're gonna win this game another time. . . ." Richard, having not yet attended a football game, remained mute, while other faculty sang with varying degrees of enthusiasm. Mostly the men mouthed words, or sang virtually under their breath. Several stood stolidly, their arms folded across their chests, lips not moving.

Finishing the fight song, Miss Grace asked if there were any requests. Someone suggested "Oh God Our Help in Ages Past," and Miss Grace sounded middle C on the piano for pitch. After the hymn Dr. Piquete requested his favorite song, "Once in Love with Amy." "As just about everyone knows, Amy is the name of our firstborn. And by the way, she called last night with news that she received an A on her Poly-Sci research project at Replet State. Mildred and I are terribly proud of her."

Miss Grace led the applause, her hands over her head. The faculty sang four more numbers before Dr. Piquete said he thought that was enough for today.

Miss Grace's eyes widened. "Are you sure, Dr. Piquete? I thought we were just warmed up."

The principal smiled. "I couldn't agree with you more, Miss Grace. However, there's been a good deal of excitement today, what with Fundy's speech. But more than that, I have another appointment downtown at the board office." Miss Grace suggested the rest of them stay for more singing, even though Dr. Piquete had to depart. But others pressed her with various reasons why they too, needed to leave.

When he arrived home from school, Luther was standing in the driveway, Johann Strauss the Younger at his side, talking to Elwood. Richard emerged from his car, and Johann dashed over to sniff his shoes before Luther called the dog.

"Your dad and I have been talking about Lucy Parlotear," Luther said. "I ran into her at the Dairy Queen couple nights ago and she's getting married again. We got to talking and one thing led to another, and she invited you and me to her wedding next

Saturday. Now your dad wants us to drag him along too, and I don't have a problem with that. He suggested we go together and buy a present for her. Your dad's a real card, Rich. Know what he suggested as a gift? A membership in the Mustard of the Month Club."

"Hey, everybody likes mustard," Elwood said. "Yellow mustard, red, brown, green—all the colors of the rainbow."

Ignoring his father, Richard furrowed his brow. "I have a slight problem with that, Luther. First of all I don't much feel like going, and Dad, here, who's not serious about the etiquette of gifting newlyweds, is clearly only interested in the reception lunch."

"Now you wait just a cotton-pickin' minute, Dickie. I bet Lucy didn't say anything about a gift when she talked to Luther.'

"Of course not, Dad. It's implied. Everybody knows that, except possibly you. You go to a wedding, you bring a gift. I don't think mustard qualifies."

Luther bent down to scratch Johann's ears. "No big deal, Rich. I'll probably go. Lucy was a good kid, even though she could hardly shut up. She hasn't changed much in that regard." He straightened up. "Say, didn't you two used to date a little?"

"They did indeed," said Elwood. "There's a woman with a head on her shoulders, if you ask me."

Richard cast an irritated glance at his father. "I won't be going to the wedding. Nothing against Lucy, but frankly, I don't know her now. Not really."

Luther shrugged. "Hey, I just thought it might be fun. There'll probably be a number of the old gang there. Folks I haven't seen since graduation"

"You go, Luther. You might have a terrific time." Richard extracted several pieces of junk mail from the box and scanned them.

Luther tossed a ball for Johann, and the dog raced down the drive in pursuit. "Say, I don't know what to make of this, but there's a story going around about some teacher stealing apples from Ray Whitsung's tree. Ray's family used to attend Dad's church way back. Geez."

"That was Dickie, Luther," Elwood said, grinding out a cigarette butt with his heel. "But don't tell nobody. Could cost him his job."

"What?"

"Aw, Dad. Don't you ever know when to shut up?"

"That's no way to talk to your father, Dickie."

"Rich?"

"It's nothing like you're thinking, Luther."

"You ever snitch apples when you were a kid, Luther?" Elwood removed another cigarette from his case, tapping it against his wrist watch.

"Sure. What kid didn't?"

"Dickie didn't. Never. Not once."

Luther looked at Richard, then back to Elwood. "So?"

"A man tries to expose his son to different experiences. You'd do the same with your own boy, Luther."

Luther emitted a brief chortle. "Not that—"

"Dad, why don't you just tell Luther exactly what happened?" Richard said, slapping the stack of junk mail against his thigh.

Elwood lighted another cigarette, and started toward the house. "Some other time, Dickie. Not now."

"Dad."

Forget it, Rich." Luther whistled for his dog. "I should be getting back. I'm expecting a call from Jezebel right about now. We'll talk later."

Richard opened a can of corned beef hash and heated it for supper. He made a pitcher of lemonade and sliced a tomato. He scooped up half the hash and put it on a plate, grabbed one slice of tomato and poured a glass of lemonade. He carried the dinner to his room, informing Elwood, slouched before the television, that supper was in the kitchen, and he could eat whenever he was ready. Then he started up the stairs.

20 minutes later the phone rang and Elwood hailed Richard. "Don't like canned hash, Dickie," Elwood said, as he handed the phone to his son. "Don't like it at all."

Richard took the phone with an impatient wave at Elwood, who did not move away.

"Fundy—you there? This is Hulot Piquete."

Making the connection now, Elwood grinned. "Pee-head Piquete," he said.

Richard cupped his hand over the speaker. "Dad, please, for crying out loud." Elwood moved away and Richard said hello.

"You say something there a second ago, Fundy?"

"No, that was Dad muttering."

"Oh yes, your father. I hope everything's ironed out with the Indians and his arborvitae. Strange though. Those natives from Fond du Lac have always struck me as most commendable folk. I wonder who's been vexing him."

"Well, it's all taken care of now."

"Good. Now I didn't want to spring this on you out of the blue, Fundy. But I've been on the phone tonight with several of the Sanguines who agree that in light of your work on Gwinnet, I ought to nominate you for membership in the group."

"Oh no, Dr. Piquete, don't do that." The desperate and shrill sound of his own voice startled him and he drew a deep breath.

"Just a formality. We make all our guest speakers honorary Sanguines. But in your case, since you are a citizen of our district, we'd be interested in posting you on the member list beyond that. You can pay your dues quarterly if that's more convenient."

"Dr. Piquete, it has nothing to do with dues. It's just that I'm not much of a joiner. I don't function well in organizations, and am generally uncomfortable—"

"With Sanguines? Don't be ridiculous, Fundy. My colleagues and I are phoning members right now to get their impression, and it should be all locked up by the time you give your talk day after tomorrow."

Richard groaned. "About that, Dr. Piquete. I'm troubled by this, and frankly, would really like to opt out of this assignment. It was one thing to talk to students, but quite another to community leaders."

Dr. Piquete laughed. "Oh, Fundy, don't underestimate yourself. Whoops, hold on, will you? There's another call coming in."

Richard groaned again and waited several minutes before Dr. Piquete addressed him again.

"Sorry about the delay, but that was someone with distressing news. I hate to tell you this, but apparently one of the Sanguines has rather vehemently nixed extending you a membership invitation, and even worse, has insisted you not deliver your speech to us. I can't imagine such a thing, Fundy. It's never happened before, and I'll have to follow up on it. Most unusual. You haven't alienated anyone, have you? I mean you haven't been arrested for anything, right?"

Richard exhaled sharply. "It's probably just as well, Dr. Piquete."

"Don't say that, Fundy. It's not just as well. Something's gone terribly amiss, and I take it as a personal slight."

"I wouldn't do that, sir." Richard felt his heart pound beneath his ribs. His tongue stuck to his alveolar ridge.

Elwood returned to the kitchen and glanced at Richard. "Say goodbye to old Pee-head, Dickie. You and me need to talk."

Chapter Seven

Elwood and Richard sat across from each other on the worn gray love seats that Rae had purchased nearly 20 years ago. Elwood was holding a glass of tomato juice.

"Dad," Richard began, "that apple tree business keeps rearing its ugly head and interfering with my life. That deputy sheriff is a member of that club I'm supposed to talk to, and he's making a scene about it. I may be in big trouble over this, and finally I can't just let things go. This arrangement isn't working, Dad. I've got to find a place of my own."

Elwood lit a cigarette and tossed the match into the fireplace. He sighed. "I don't like to hear you talk like that, Dickie. I mean, it'd be one thing if you were married and off raising a family. I don't see any reason why, since you're not, you shouldn't be available to look after your old man, whose health ain't all that good."

"Dad, your health isn't in danger. Sure, you smoke too much, but on balance, you're in decent shape for a man your age."

Elwood sipped tomato juice. He frowned and burped softly, then shook his head. "I'm at a critical age, Dickie. Check out the obituaries some time. Lotsa guys younger'n me are dropping like flies. Guys who were little kids when I was in high school are kickin' the old bucket, buyin' the farm. Under present circumstances, I don't think it's asking too much for you to be available. I'm not chargin' you rent, for one thing. You get a chance to save some money, maybe build up a little nest egg, and who knows, maybe you can find a woman who'll have you again. I mean, you only got one strike against you, Dickie, not two or three. You got a couple swings left, and I'm backin' you up all the way."

"The point is not whether I get married again, but whether I can keep this job. Right now, you're not helping me with that."

Elwood finished the tomato juice in one swallow, set down his glass took a long drag on the cigarette. "Job ain't everything, Dickie. When the curtain comes down on your life, you just wanna be remembered for the job you had? Life's more'n a job, Dickie. Life, as Dr. Incapace says, is like swingin' on a star." Elwood snuffed out his cigarette. "I don't know what the hell that's supposed to mean, but I know this—you make impressions, Dickie. Life's all about makin' impressions so you'll be remembered. And it seems that in these last days of my life I'm tryin' to catch up on makin' them impressions. And it also seems to me that you'd be a little more accommodating when I try to catch up on lost time as my own rope is runnin' out. It's my wish to make an impression after I'm gone." He paused, cleared his throat. "I wanna go out with my head hangin' high. You promised to mail me all over the country, remember, Dickie?"

"Yeah, I remember. But it seems to be asking too much for you to leave me out of your impression-making. I'm very uncomfortable with this, Dad."

"Don't be, Dickie. Impressions count big time."

"Dad, what is so important that you need to talk to me right now? It couldn't be about impressing people. Because frankly, the impressions you're talking about are pretty negative."

"Sorry to hear you say that, Dickie-boy." Elwood stood. "I guess maybe now isn't the right time to deal with the matter I wanted to bring up." He interlocked his fingers and slowly twisted them. "It's one of them unresolved issues, Dickie, that I gotta resolve pretty soon. I mean, if you don't get the unresolved stuff in your life resolved while you're still alive, they sure as squat don't get resolved after you get put in the ground. 'Course in my case I won't be in the ground. I'll be in them manila envelopes."

"I'm sorry this isn't working between us. I need my own space. You do too Dad. I'll still check in on you, you know that."

"Oh hell, Dickie, you think you need to go, you go. I don't know—I just wish there was somethin' I could do."

"You've already done enough, Dad. Let's just leave it at that."

The next day at school, Dr. Piquete apologized to Richard for having to withdraw the Sanguine Society invitation, and asked for Richard's notes. "It's incumbent upon me to give the talk then, Fundy. I'll of course credit you for the yeoman task you performed in putting it all together. I may even chide our people for this untoward treatment."

Richard swallowed. "I know what this is all about, Dr. Piquete.

And it really isn't worth anybody getting upset over. You have met my father. You know he's been something of a concern to me, to say nothing of a trial. But he's my father, and I stick by him."

"Where are you taking me, Fundy?" The principal removed his glasses, fogged the lenses with his breath and wiped them with a clean, ironed handkerchief.

"The reason why that deputy, Whitsung, didn't want me to speak is because, regarding that incident the other day about somebody snitching apples from his tree. I'm afraid I was sort of involved in that. It was Dad, actually, but I was there and could have been implicated as an accessory. It's been terribly embarrassing, and finally to put an end to speculation, I've decided to come clean."

The principal was frowning and rocking heel to toe. "I see." Then after several seconds, said, "No, Fundy. I don't see. I don't get it. You and your father were out behaving like mischievous children stealing apples?"

"Well yes and no. That is—"

"Excuse me, Fundy. I'm having trouble with this. Were you stealing apples or were you not stealing apples?" The principal's face had reddened, and his jaw tightened. His hands opened and clenched rhythmically against his thighs.

"I can truthfully say I didn't touch a single apple. It was Dad's idea of a stupid joke or something. I can't explain it. It's just the way he is. And I feel a sort of responsibility for him. He hasn't been himself, really, since Mother died."

Dr. Piquete scratched his jaw. "That's been quite some time, hasn't it?"

"Eight years."

"That should be enough time to get your act back together, it seems to me." Dr. Piquete looked expectantly at Richard.

"I suppose that depends."

"Depends? Depends on what? Good heavens, Fundy, doesn't the man realize that his son is a teacher in this community, and as such is held to something of a higher standard, and that stealing apples is quite likely an impeachable offense? To say nothing of damaging not only your credibility, but the credibility of all educators everywhere."

"I'm sorry, Dr. Piquete. I can only hope something like this doesn't happen again."

"I think you'll have to do better than hope, Fundy." Dr. Piquete stood facing Richard, rocking back on his heels, his arms folded, his lips pulled downward.

"I'm looking for an apartment of my own. It's been a trial living at home with Dad."

Dr. Piquete blinked. "You mean you'd leave your father in the lurch? You can't do that. Why here's the man who supported you during your formative years. He and your mother brought you up to be the chap you are today. You don't just abandon such a man, Fundy. You say he's a bit of a queer duck, and I'm not about to disagree, but at the same time, since you've no other family responsibilities, you've a duty to tend to this man. Don't leave him, Fundy. For all the difficulties an aged parent brings to our lives, when we are there for them, there are uncounted rewards in the sacrifice. I know; I speak from experience. Mildred and I took her mother into our home, where she dwelt among us for nearly 10 years. Was I happy with this arrangement, Fundy? I'm not ashamed to admit I was not. The old harridan was a real load. Intruded in our lives, got under our skin." Dr. Piquete grimaced. "Nothing was good enough. She carped constantly, insisted on a special diet. Bland foods, and so forth. She was always stopped up and needed enemas two or three times a week. If she had her way, she wanted one every single day. I told her she should increase her fiber intake, but did she listen? I wanted to tear my hair. But I did not complain. I did my duty to that woman, and am grateful for it."

Richard sighed before speaking. "So your sacrifice was beneficial, Dr. Piquete?"

The principal brightened, and he clapped Richard on the shoulder. "Without question, Fundy. She left us nearly a half million dollars when she passed on. That was more than a minor benefit in my book. So these things have a way of working themselves out, you see. I hope you'll consider my advice on this matter. But do try to keep a lid on Mr. Fundy's capers. Above all, we must not expose the school to embarrassment."

"Nobody knows that better than I."

Dr. Piquete nodded. "I would certainly expect nothing less, Fundy."

"In any case, I have an appointment directly after school to check an apartment in the Bella Vita complex. That's not even a mile from school. I could walk to work, get a little exercise before and after school."

"Not the Bella Vita, Fundy," the principal said, vigorously shaking his head. "You don't want to situate yourself so close. You'd have problems. A few kids—the bad apples that always seem to rise like cream—would likely vandalize your car in the parking lot, for instance. Or another resident's car, believing it to be yours. Which would be far worse. You'd be responsible for bringing school problems into the lives of ordinary citizens. And, need I remind you, these are the people with the purse strings, so to speak. They vote, Fundy. And they vote on important bond issues affecting the future of our schools. And rather directly, your own future, Fundy. If you're all-fired determined to abandon your father, at least find someplace a bit further from school. You can walk from there. The advantage is you couldn't meander down the street, but you'd move at a brisk clip, which is far superior for conditioning the body. Especially during the winter.

"Oh, and one other thing. Forgive me if my comments seem ill-mannered, but you have struck me as a man of some fragility, Fundy. I admit to appreciating the hale and vigorous lifestyle myself, and I appreciate that in others as well. But to each his own. However, hearkening to your *heartsick* condition, may I suggest that you take up a daily habit of walking. I have, over the years, done my utmost to encourage our Button Gwinnet family to engage both body and mind, and have, on numerous occasions, urged our faculty to walk more. I know it can be difficult at times, especially when the air outside smells of effluent. It's the paper mills doing that, and it can be unpleasant, but I have it on good authority the odor isn't toxic. You should walk, Fundy, and condition yourself to ignore the paper mill odors. You'll be fit as a fiddle, and there'll be no more of this heartsick nonsense. I hope you'll take this little suggestion. You'll be much better off for it."

Richard's shoulders sagged. "Yes, Dr. Piquete. Thank you for your concern."

Dr. Piquete nodded and gripped Richard's elbow. "That's the spirit, Fundy. Good man." He nodded again and strode down the hall, pausing to check his watch before turning into the office.

Richard spent several hours after class on Wednesday and Thursday looking at apartments, but found none satisfactory. Elwood said he doubted Richard would find anything as suitable as living at home, rent-free. "At least you got somebody to shoot the breeze with, Dickie. You get yourself cooped up in one of them skimpy apartments, why all's you got is your radio or TV. That's no substitute for a real live person in your life. I'm surprised you don't figure that out for yourself."

On Friday after Richard returned home, Elwood offered to take him out for dinner. "We'll get bucked up and out of the dumps, Dickie. They make a real good fried chicken at Art's Place. Some cold slaw and French fries with the skin on and a couple ice cold beers, why you'll be tall in the saddle. It'll be my treat, this time, Dickie. Honest." Elwood crossed his heart. "Hope to die, Dickie," he added.

Hoskar Bunting noticed Richard and Elwood enter, and grinning broadly, ambled toward them. "Lemme buy you birds a couple beers," he said, making a playful jab at Elwood's midsection.

"I could go for a highball," Elwood said.

Hoskar laughed. "Hey, I said beer. Arthur's been raisin' his prices somethin' fierce. Four bucks for a martini."

"Well then, beer it is, and thank you very much, Hoskar," Elwood said.

Emil Slepka sidled over, holding a glass of white wine. "Hey, looka this, guys. Me drinkin' a pretty tasty pwee fussy, or somethin' like that. Arthur pointed out it don't have that tannin taste you hear so much about these days. Light and fruity. Between you and me I'd as soon have a Dr. Pepper with my fried chicken. But how're you gonna sophisticate yourself if you don't drink what the hoi polloi likes? You guys eatin' tonight?"

Elwood nodded and started to speak, but was interrupted by Hoskar. "Emil, the hoi polloi is us. You meant to say hoity-toity."

"Maybe," said Emil, tasting the wine again. He resumed talking but was soon drowned out by a crew setting up risers in the small atrium of the bar.

"Arthur's got a chorus comin' in tonight," somebody hollered. "The One Never Knows, Do One? Chorale. They sing a lot of Fats Waller, but also Scarlotti and Charlie Mingus. Ought to be a blast."

Ignoring the announcement, Hoskar grinned and said. "Got another commission last week, Elwood. Lucy Parlotear—gal that runs that Lean Mean Mamas health club wants me to come up with some kind of fitness theme for her place. Ain't a big commission, but hells bells, who'd have thought that I'd be gettin' commissions of any kind? In my day, you used to sometimes get the low bid on a job. But now that I'm an artiste, I get me commissions. And it's usually for a pretty high bid too. Go figure."

"Well good for you, Hoskar." Elwood extended his hand to Hoskar as a bartender set beers before him and Richard.

"Yes, congratulations," Richard said. "And thanks for the beer."

"Don't mention it," Hoskar replied. "So anyway, this Lucy Parlotear's gettin' married tomorrow. Second time, she tells me. Well good luck, I says. She wants this piece done by the time she comes back from the honeymoon. Goin' on some cruise, I understand. Shoot, Elwood, I could knock out that baby practically overnight. But y'know what? When you're an artist, you gotta take time. The client likes to think you slave over a piece for weeks or months. So my agent says, just let 'em think what they wanna think, and so long as their check's good, not to worry my pretty little head over it." Hoskar shrugged. "Anyhow, she's invited me to the wedding. I might go. Open bar at the reception. Can't beat that."

"Dickie used to date Lucy back in high school. There's a gal who's got her act together." Elwood sipped his beer and scowled. "If he'da played his cards right, it'd be him marrying Lucy, and he'da been on easy street. Woman with her own business and all. She could of taken care of you, Dickie. Your worries would have been over."

"Guess it wasn't meant to be, Dad." Richard smiled at Hoskar.

"Well, I don't know where you think you'll find another high class female around these parts, Dickie. Those worth having are all spoken for, and so are a lot of them that ain't worth a rat's fart."

Hoskar poked Richard's arm with his fist. "Hell, Elwood, the boy's young yet. Lotsa fish in the creek. What do you think, Emil?"

"Makes no never mind to me. I had enough trouble pickin' out a wife of my own. I ain't sayin' nothin' about nobody else's old lady." He sipped his wine, then grinned. "As long as you pick one from the upper crust, young fella. Leave the hoi polloi alone. Hitch your saddle to a star would be my advice."

"Ain't nothin' wrong with hoi polloi, but Dickie's snake-bit from his first experience," Elwood said. "But like I says, that shouldn't discourage a man. Cripes, Hoskar, remember that fella from back in the '50s—Tommy Manville? How many times did he find a wife? Ten or thirteen, I betcha. 'Course he had the moola for alimony, and I ain't suggestin' Dickie marries over and over again, but at the same time if at first you don't succeed you don't up and quit."

"When the time's right, Dad."

"That's part of the problem, Dickie. You think you got all the time in the world. But as you and me know, Hoskar, you don't have hardly no time for nothin' when it gets right down to it."

Hoskar Bunting stared at his beer. "Ain't it the truth. And like Dr. Incapace says, a man's life's full of unresolved issues. Why, when you think of it, you hardly got time to take care of them. You know me, Elwood. I mean, when I let my life get cluttered up with all that crap from when I was a union steward, I could hardly see straight. 'Course, I was hittin' the sauce a bit in them days too. But I'll say this for those times—it got me outta my marriage. Wife divorced me 'cause I was an old soak." He chuckled. "As luck would have it, I became an artist right after that and started makin' scratch hand over fist." He laughed again. "She couldn't touch one thin dime of it. So it all works out for the best." He shook his head and chuckled softly. "'Course, that ain't nothing. My youngest brother, Francis, now he takes the cake when it comes to shedding women. Yessir, Francis, he's maybe a couple quarts low, if you catch my drift." Hoskar tapped his temple with a forefinger.

"But he made some good money as a machinist. Anyhow, Ada, his second wife, took off one day. Couldn't stand livin' in the messes

Francis was making. He went through a phase there where he thought he was an inventor tryin' out all kinds of patents and all.

"None of them came to squat. Anyways, ol' Ada who wasn't much of a looker to begin with, gets lonesome and wants to come back. Fine, Francis says. But you know what he done while she was gone? He renovated the whole damn garage. Put in a batting cage and had one of them pitching machines installed. Installed heating vents so he could be out there in his shorts all winter. He musta been about 50 years old then, for cryin' out loud. He tells Ada he's gonna practice all winter in the batting cage with that pitching machine and he's by God gonna go down to Florida come spring and be a designated hitter for a big league team. He really thinks he can do it too. Well, that soured Ada, of course, and she up and went. That was the end of that. Francis bought a pair of spikes and took a dozen bats to Florida that February, and tried to get Seattle to give him a shot. He always liked Ken Griffey, Jr. you know. Wanted to play on his team. Said they could win a pennant with the two of them." Hoskar laughed. "Seattle had the cops run him off. Figured he was a looney. Which he was, but he wasn't dangerous. I mean, he never even played baseball when he was in school. The damn fool really believed he could play the game. But hell, a 50 year-old man ain't gonna make nobody's baseball team." Hoskar took a swallow of beer. "Know what he's been up to lately? He's tryin' to be a pool hustler. Couple years back, he don't know a cue ball from a side pocket. But you can't tell him nothin', so anyway I had to loan him $300 last month otherwise he says he was gonna get his face rearranged by some dudes in Duluth because he couldn't cover his losses, you see. He lives there now because they got more places for him to play. West end saloons. Kinda rough on old Francis, who never was fancy with his dukes."

Hoskar looked at Richard. "Listen, kid, you ever consider seeing Dr. Incapace yourself?"

Richard shook his head. "Never."

"Dickie thinks he's a quack, Hoskar," Elwood said as a waitress came over to take their dinner order. "Two-a these," he said, pointing to the fried chicken on the menu.

Hoskar chuckled again. "Shoot, lotsa people say the same thing about me. But talk is cheap. Can't really hurt you. I mean, it ain't like a knee to the castanets, as the doc likes to say. He's been a big help to me and your daddy, young man. I wanted Francis to get an appointment, but Francis thinks he's as normal as bread pudding. I give up trying. And I know Doc would get Emil straightened around too, but 'a course, that'd take a helluva long time." Hoskar and Elwood laughed, but Emil stared mutely at his glass.

Richard lifted his shoulders and shook his head. He put both hands around his pilsner.

"You don't have to say nothin', Dickie. Your puss lets everybody know what you're thinkin'." Elwood drained his glass and signaled for another.

Hoskar and Emil left to join other friends who were assuming positions near the risers as the One Never Knows, Do One? Chorale filed in. Elwood and Richard were ignoring the music—which began with Wagner's Soldiers March from Faust, and soon the waitress brought platters of food for Richard and Elwood. Before they began eating, Elwood tapped Richard's hand. "Ya notice that waitress, Dickie? I think she's interested in you. Kinda looked at you in a lingerin' sort of way, if you know what I mean. Seems like a nice gal, Dickie. Maybe you ought to see what time she gets off work tonight."

"Dad, please, for heaven's sake."

"You a snob now, Dickie? Think a waitress is beneath you? Never mind what Emil says. That ain't the way I raised you. These waitresses today run their buns off, so they're in good shape. Our gal here looks pretty trim to me. Probably 35-40. If you're lucky she don't have kids. That there woman could probably teach you a thing or two about music, art, and literature." He signaled the waitress.

"Dad, just drop it, okay."

The waitress hurried to Elwood. "Yes, sir?"

Elwood studied the waitress's name tag. "Uh, Charlotte, old girl, me and the boy here were just havin' a little discussion. And I'm countin' on you to settle the matter for us. Who wrote 'The Barber of Seville?'"

"Rossini," she quickly replied. "Libretto by Sterbini, based on the comedy by Beaumarchais." She smiled, stepped back and began singing, "Figaro—Figaro-Figaro-Figaro. . . ."

"See there, Dickie. Most people would say Mozart. They don't know squat. Mozart wrote 'The Marriage of Figaro,' which continues the story ol' Rossini partly told. Now, you gotta admit there ain't many waitresses who'd know that, Dickie." Elwood looked up at a smiling Charlotte and said, "Thank you very much." Then he nudged his son. "Give this lady a couple dollars, Dickie."

As Richard tipped her, Elwood wrenched a drumstick from the thigh of his chicken and gestured with it. "Dickie, I'm not gonna be around forever. Sooner'n you think, you're gonna be all alone in this world with nobody to look after you. Now a waitress here, she probably won't be as demanding as whatsername, your ex." He took a large bite of drumstick and chewed, eyeballing Richard over the tops of his glasses.

Richard broke off a wing and nibbled it. "You're right about one thing, Dad. Good chicken." Then as the opening notes from "'Round Midnight" sounded, Richard paused to look at the Chorale. There stepping off the riser assuming a soloist's position near the director was Marvella Grace. Miss Grace eased into a scat riff, a seamless effort, though she stood with hands clasped at her bosom as she sang. Through the throng she noticed Richard and broke into a broad smile.

When the chorale concluded its set, she hurried to Richard's and Elwood's table. "Well, well, Mr. Fundy, isn't this a surprise."

"Yes, Miss Grace, it certainly is. I had no idea."

She glanced from Richard to Elwood. "One is always searching, ever seeking to expand one's horizons. Don't you do that yourself, sir?" she said, looking at Elwood.

"Oh, Miss Grace, this is my father, Elwood Fundy. Dad, Miss Grace teaches vocal music at Button Gwinnet."

"Pleased to meetcha, Gracie."

"Miss Grace—Marvella, Dad, not Gracie."

Miss Grace chuckled. "It doesn't matter one little bit. I rather like Gracie. Reminds me of Gracie Allen, who always made me laugh. Actually, it was my father who laughed so hard, but I loved my father, and so she gave me joy for that reason. You don't think I resemble Gracie Allen, do you?"

Elwood gave Miss Grace a once-over. "Nah, she was just a little bitty thing, if I remember. You got a lot more meat on your bones."

"Dad."

"Why thank you, Mr. Fundy." Miss Grace beamed.

"So you're a friend of Dickie's. You wanna join us for a little libation?"

"My, how very kind. How very sweet, really. I'd love to, thank you so much, but can't. You see, our bus departs momentarily. But a rain check would be awfully nice."

"Sure, Gracie. Next time," said Elwood, returning to his chicken.

❖❖❖❖❖

Shortly after one p.m. on Saturday, Luther arrived to pick up Elwood for Lucy Parlotear's wedding. After briefly attempting to persuade Richard to join them, the two drove off in Luther's Honda.

Richard had been correcting papers at the kitchen table when the phone rang.

"Rich, I hate to bother, but you better get over here quick. Your dad is—well, you better get right over."

"Oh, Geez," Richard gasped, hanging up, and dashing for his car. Park Community Church of All the Saints was only five minutes away. Richard made it in less than four, and dashed into the sanctuary to find Elwood, dressed in a checked sport coat with maroon slacks and white patent leather shoes, standing in the pew near the middle, apparently haranguing the preacher. Luther, standing in the rear of the church, grabbed Richard.

"Thank God," he whispered. "He's disrupted the service. This is just awful, Rich."

"What happened?"

"The minister got to where he said if anyone objected to the union he should speak now or hold his peace. Your father decided to speak. He made a big deal about the groom being disabled."

Moaning, Richard followed Luther down the side aisle to Elwood's row. "And besides that," Elwood was saying, "you'll be waitin' on this fella hand and foot. Now for all I know, he might be a wonderful man, but Lucy, you're fit and strong—"

"Dad!" Richard clutched his father's sleeve. He noticed the congregation staring at him and Elwood; the wedding party, mouths agape, looking on in shocked disbelief.

Elwood glanced at his son and pushed him away. The wheelchair-bound groom held his head in his hands and the bride's face crimsoned. An obviously distraught minister adjusted his collar and raised his hand. Lucy left the altar and marched toward Elwood.

"Shut up, you," she rasped.

"If you'll be so kind as to be seated," the preacher intoned, his brow furrowed.

"I'm simply sayin' that there are other options in this life, Lucy, and you shouldn't be rushin' into something—especially considering this man's condition. You can see he'll require a lot of attention. I got a healthy fella right here." Elwood pointed to his son. "Now you take Dickie here—"

"Dickie?" Lucy roared. "Dickie?"

"Dad, please," Richard gasped, and tried to step between his father and Lucy "Lucy, I—" he started before toppling over after a stiff right hand from the bride caught him on the left temple, knocking him back into the pew. He didn't move for several seconds, finally struggling to sit up. Voices of his father, Luther, Lucy, and the pastor emerged through the intense ringing in his ears, and he thought he heard Lucy shouting and Luther pleading with her not to hit Elwood.

Then Luther was pulling Richard to his feet and leading him down the aisle. Lucy had Elwood in a hammerlock while she ushered him toward the back of the church, and the minister followed closely behind, murmuring, "Oh, lord, oh, dear."

"You just get lost and stay lost," Lucy snarled after shoving Elwood through the exit. "And you." She shot daggers at Richard as she returned to her groom who had wheeled himself to the rear of the church.

Richard, trailed by Luther, woozily passed through the door, and was stopped by the minister. He gripped Richard's shoulder and whispered, "We may question the events that have unfolded here, but I believe there's a purpose in everything. In this instance, it may force you to attend the obvious needs of this wretched man I assume is your father. You have my prayers in this sordid undertaking."

Richard glanced at him, then vomited on the sidewalk.

As Elwood slid into the passenger seat in Luther's Honda, Luther put Richard in the back seat, then drove to a convenience store and purchased a bag of ice, instructing Richard to hold it to his bruised temple.

"Mark my words," Elwood said, as Luther started the car, "one day Lucy will think back on this day and figure, by golly, ol' Elwood Fundy was right. I don't often speak out like that, but I just hate to see a young woman throw away her life, for crying out loud. Why on earth would a fit and strong gal like that want to marry a crippled fella?"

"Shut up, Dad," Richard moaned. "For once, please shut up."

"How's the head, Rich?" said Luther.

"I'll live."

"Damn, that gal can throw a punch," said Elwood, shaking his head. "If it'd of been me she'd nailed, I don't know if I'da been on my feet yet. There for a minute I thought maybe she was gonna run me all the way back to Cloquet and chuck me off the Main Street bridge. I'm not much of a swimmer, you know." He chuckled. "Hell, I didn't know you could take a wallop like that, Dickie. I never would have—"

"Dad, geez, take a hint, will you?" Richard moaned again and repositioned the bag of ice.

"Maybe we should just let Rich rest." Luther forced a smile at Elwood.

"You're probably right, Luther. I'm sorry about this, Dickie. Really. I didn't mean for anybody to get nailed like that. I believe she was aiming at me, but you got in the way. Or she's got lousy aim. One or the other. Thing is gals ain't used to scrappin' like that. Which, as it turned out, was lucky for me, and of course, not so lucky for you, Dickie. A head-shot like that can leave you wobbly and sick for a couple days. Sometimes you hear of prizefighters spending two-three days in bed after they've been knocked out. Probably be the same with you. Ya lost your cookies back at the church, so I wouldn't recommend you eat anything for the rest of the day."

"Dad!" Richard wailed.

"Ooops, sorry, Dickie." Elwood cleared his throat, then asked Luther if it would be all right to light a cigarette.

"It probably would upset Rich, Elwood."

Elwood was tapping the cigarette against his watch, but he put it back in the pack. "Geez, I hope this don't last too long, Luther. I always smoke in my own house."

Luther nodded, then spoke softly. "He'll be okay after a bit. Let him get some rest, and he'll be fine."

Elwood grunted, then turned around to look at Richard, whose eyes were closed. Water from the ice bag had trickled down onto his collar, soaking it. Elwood faced front. "Ice melted and now Dickie's shirt is wet."

Luther nodded and pressed a finger to his lips, and the rest of the trip was silent.

After Luther assisted Richard into the house, he drove home. Elwood started a pot of tea. "Tea goes down easy on a bad gut, Dickie," he said. His son, still pressing the ice bag to his face, lay on the living room sofa. "I'll bring you a cup when it's done."

Richard moaned.

The doorbell chimed—the opening lines to "When You Wish Upon A Star," that Rae had installed years earlier. But the apparatus had worn down and several notes buzzed instead of chimed. Neither Elwood nor Richard moved to open the door and the bell sounded again.

"I'm busy with the tea, Dickie," Elwood called. "You wanna see who that is?"

Richard struggled to his feet and shuffled to the door as the bell rang a third time.

He opened the door, blinked against the sun. "You birds can't stay out of trouble, can you?" said a sour-faced Deputy Whitsung. "You jokers take the cake in my book." He held up an arrest warrant.

Chapter Eight

Deputy Whitsung seemed pleased as he cuffed Richard and Elwood before putting them in his squad car and driving them to headquarters. All during the ride he harangued about the renegade nature of schoolteachers these days, and how they, more than anything else, had turned the public away from supporting education. "It's jokers like you who spoil things for the few good teachers left in this world. I really feel sorry for guys like Roscoe Hammerlee, who's been retired five, ten years. Helluva football coach and helluva man. Learned more lessons from him on the field than in any classroom. Coach used to run us 'till we barfed, but by God, it made us tough. Now what do we get? Buncha candy-asses who sneak around swiping apples and disrupting weddings. Hell, wouldn't surprise me one damn bit if there's teachers stealing kids' bicycles from the racks in front of school." He shook his head, then glanced at Elwood.

"And you, I tried giving you a break the other day, but was that a mistake. I mean, it was you who raised this meatball to become a sneak thief." He rolled down his window and spat. "Anyhow, at least you're not a teacher."

Elwood bore the ignominy in silence, and he and Richard posted $500 bonds for disturbing the peace, then were released. Elwood asked if the deputy or one of the other officers would drive them back home.

"Are you nuts?" Whitsung said, glaring at Elwood before he returned his attention to papers on his desk. "Get outta here before I arrest you again. I can think of some charge, by damn."

"Dad, come on," Richard said, after Elwood paused and seemed about to take up the issue again with the officer.

A cab ride and $24.65 later, Richard and Elwood were back in their Mister Lane home, where the interior was redolent of fried bacon not quite gone rank and stale cigarette smoke. Elwood lit up, sat in his recliner and started thumbing a copy of *Contemporary Art*. "Good to be home, huh, Dickie?" He appeared engrossed in the magazine. "About time for supper, don'tcha think? Hell, after the day we had, we should treat ourselves to steak. Porterhouse or ribeye. Baked potato, French bread, tossed salad, bottle of cold duck. Whaddaya say, Dickie? You up for that? Me, I'm hungrier'n a coot." He chuckled.

Richard sat slumped in the sofa, gingerly fingering his bruise.

"Little joke there, Dickie-boy. I said I was hungrier'n a coot. Coots ain't big eaters, Dickie. Least I don't think they are. Not much size to 'em."

Richard moaned.

"Head still botherin' you, Dickie?" Elwood lowered the magazine.

Richard slowly stood. "Dad, shut up!" he said. He pressed his right hand to his temple and started for the stairs. He entered his room, closing the door behind him and dropped on his bed. Ten minutes later he phoned Luther, explaining what happened, their arrest by Deputy Whitsung, and the posting of bond. "This will get into the *Journal* and *Pine Knot* both, Luther," Richard said. "Probably even hit the *Duluth News Tribune*, with my luck. My job is in jeopardy here."

"Rich, for what it's worth, you can't get fired for something like this. My hunch is charges'll probably be dismissed. At worst, you get a small fine. It's nothing, Rich. *Nada*. Certainly it isn't grounds for dismissal. The incident had absolutely nothing to do with your teaching."

"Yeah, but this isn't a large community. I can't function as a teacher here if I'm hauled into court for disturbing the peace. Besides, I didn't disturb the peace, Luther. I wouldn't give a damn if Dad got a few days in jail. Might teach him a lesson. I'm having a real hard time with our lives. I made a huge mistake coming back to live in this house."

"Look, Rich, I know you're down right now. I appreciate that. Why don't I swing by in a few minutes and take you out for a drink? If you don't want to, fine. I understand. It's your call."

"The last thing I need right now is to be in the house with Dad. I'll be outside waiting for you."

Richard washed his face in the bathroom, put on a fresh shirt, went downstairs and grabbed a jacket. He barged through the door, ignoring Elwood's inquiry. "Hey, Dickie-boy, where you goin'?" He hurried to the end of the driveway, but did not turn around, as Elwood watched him from the open doorway. He could smell smoke from Elwood's cigarette in the breeze. He jammed his hands in his jacket pocket and waited at the top of the driveway for Luther, who arrived about five minutes later.

Richard got in and leaned his head against the window. Luther drove along a County Highway RR for several minutes before speaking. "Rich, I decided to stay with my original scheme for tonight, but if you don't like it, just say the word. I can take you home, and it's no problem."

"Thanks. I'll be okay."

"This'll be different. You ever hear of ferret-legging? It's a sport, if you want to call it that, comes from Yorkshire. I used to think it must be French. They've got some doozies in France. They have this one they call bull-in-the-swimming pool. Crazy. There's like a kid's wading pool, and you score when you can get this raging bull to get in there with you. They have another sport where they put a bull in a soccer match. You get a breakaway, heading for the goal, but whoa—here comes the bull. Do you shoot or run for your life?" He chuckled. "Ever been to the Waltzing Walleye Taverna on Perch Lake?"

Richard shook his head.

Luther nodded. "Should prove interesting."

"What's ferret-legging?" Richard asked absently, resting his head against the window again.

❖❖❖❖❖

On the roof of the Waltzing Walleye Taverna was a large pink neon-lighted outline of a grinning pike. A cigar was positioned in the fish's mouth; one eye winked as the light alternated from open to shut, while the fish, standing on its tail, undulated.

A scant handful of women mingled among the male throng inside the bar. The Waltzing Walleye was decorated in the requisite outdoor motif, the centerpiece being a large moose head over the bar, supported by mounted ducks and geese, stringers of lacquered largemouth bass and walleyed pike. Neon beer signs illuminated scenes of hunters and anglers in action and in repose. In the center of the barroom was a small ring, about four feet square. Near the ring were three wire cages holding ferrets.

Amidst the badinage, several contestants stood silently at the bar downing shots of bourbon and eyeing the caged animals.

Luther brought Richard a large brandy. "Industrial strength," he said, placing the glass before Richard. "Just the ticket for what ails you."

Richard took a swallow of the drink and winced slightly. "So what gives here, Luther? What do they do with the critters?"

"Let it be a surprise, Rich."

Richard grunted and took a gulp from his glass. His gaze swept the room. "I don't know, Luther, this doesn't look like your kind of place. It's a little, shall we say, *declasse?*"

"Hey, that's its charm. Sort of a downscale Art's Place. Not a fern anywhere in sight. And a dollar to a donut the bartender couldn't mix a Pimm's Cup if his life depended on it."

Richard downed his drink and Luther signaled for another. Meanwhile, a beefy, middle-aged man with muttonchops, wearing the striped shirt of a sports referee, climbed into the ring. A wiry, long-haired, bespectacled man about 30 years old stood near the caged ferrets and appeared to be talking to the animals in a low voice.

In the ring, the referee held up his hands and shouted for silence. He said they'd be getting underway in a moment. Because ferrets were nervous creatures, he announced the establishment didn't want drink orders shouted during the competition, so anyone a little short should be replenished now or shut the hell up.

The din quieted, and he went on to say that only five athletes had entered this evening's competition, but since this was an open tournament, there were spaces available for others. Anyone interested should see Frank at the bar to sign up.

"What about it, Rich?" Luther said around a laugh. "You could go back to school Monday and try to sell the athletic department on ferret-legging as a varsity sport."

Richard nodded and stared at his drink.

Luther pulled him to his feet. "We have to get closer to get a good look." They wormed through the crowd and stood about 10 feet from the ring. The ferret master opened a cage and removed an animal. He gently stroked it, held it close to his face and whispered.

To no one in particular, an onlooker pointed to the ferret and announced, "That there one's a ball biter."

"They bite?" Richard said.

"And scratch. Do they ever scratch," said a fan, empathetically dancing and grimacing at the thought of a ferret probing his nether regions.

The ring announcer explained the rules to the crowd. "As most of you know, contestants can't have underwear. Naked as jaybirds under their trousers. Also, we differ a little from our friends in England. We only use one ferret, not two. We're new at this sport, so it'll take some time for our people to try two ferrets. Now the world record for a double down the trousers is an amazing five hours. No one in our competitions has gone more than 90 seconds with just one ferret. But you never can tell, hey? In fact, any contestant managing to last an hour wins $1000 and a case of beer a week. Without further adieu, our first contestant," said the official, as a young college man, cheered by his fraternity brothers, removed his shirt and climbed into the ring wearing sweat pants.

Two men tied shoelaces around the bottom of each leg, then stood back. The top of the sweat pants was loosened, and the attendant entered the ring with a ferret. The contestant blanched as the animal was inserted into his pants, then froze, yowled, and executed about a dozen acrobatic kicks, before falling on his back, hollering. The attendant removed the ferret and the referee announced a time of six seconds.

"Hey, that shouldn't be too hard to beat," the referee roared into his megaphone.

Several other contestants let ferrets scurry about their loins with 12 seconds holding first place.

Suddenly, Richard, having downed two large brandies, told Luther he wanted to give this ferret-legging a shot. "Rich, don't be an idiot. You could sacrifice your tool or a testicle, for God's sake."

"I can do this thing," he said, burping. "I know it."

Richard registered, and after donning someone's sweat pants, stumbled into the ring. Rivulets of sweat ran off his face. The ferret master said, "Try not to move around too much. They don't like to be jostled."

Richard managed to remain more or less stationary for 25 seconds, before tearing at the sweat pants and releasing the ferret. He was declared winner, and his photo was taken as he was presented a check for $100 and a case of Sodbuster, a local brew that retailed for nine dollars.

Onlookers crowded into the ring to congratulate him, and marvel at his ability to withstand the prowlings and scratchings of the ferret. "I was lucky I didn't draw the ball-biter," Richard said to an operative from the local community access cable channel. He left the ring and quickly drained another brandy, courtesy of the management.

"I don't know, Rich," said Luther tentatively.

"Don't know what?" Richard said, flopping into a nearby booth and putting his head on the table.

"This might not have been such a good idea."

"Won a hundred bucks and a case of rotten beer. Besides, I hardly felt a thing." He looked up at Luther without lifting his head from the table. "Proved I was an athlete, didn't I?"

"I suppose you proved something, Rich. What, I'm not exactly sure. But for what it's worth, congratulations. You did win the hundred bucks, and that'll come in handy, I suppose."

Richard burped. "Siddown, Luther. Have another drink. Celebrate, dammit. I won the trophy and I feel like celebrating."

He lowered his head to the table, resting it on a crooked arm. "On the other hand, maybe I don't feel all that good."

Luther nodded. "That's what I was thinking. It might be a good idea to get you home."

"Don't have a home, Luther," Richard said as he tried to stand. He fell against Luther, who steadied him and brought him to the car.

"It was just plain stupid, if you ask me, Dickie." Elwood was standing over Richard's bed on Sunday morning. Richard moaned, and without opening his eyes, rolled away from his father. "If you hadn't won the hundred clams, it'd have been about the dumbest thing you ever did. I suppose it's your business if you never want to father children, but them ferrets have sharp teeth. One little nip and it could have been all over, Dickie. I'm surprised at you. Beats hell out of me why you'd try that idiotic sport.

"'Course, you come back here drunker'n a skunk, which ain't like you, neither. You developin' mental problems or what, Dickie? I mean, here I am, practically at the end of my days, and I got to deal with somebody else's lunatic notions. I got problems of my own—enough to last me well beyond the grave, Dickie. Whoops—no grave for me—envelopes, I mean. But you get the drift."

Richard moaned again.

"Gonna upchuck, Dickie? You better get into the john. I sure as hell ain't gonna clean up after you. You're old enough to know better, Dickie, and that's all I'm gonna say about this." He paused for a moment, scratching his stubbled jaw. "Dickie, what can you tell me about this old biddy Gracie that teaches with you? She come by last night with a crock of soup. Smelled like cabbage, which as you know, I don't eat, so after she left I gave it to the disposal. She invited me to some music session too. In a moment of weakness I said yes."

Richard moaned. "She probably is hot for you, Dad." He turned his face into his pillow.

"Huh? You puttin' me on, Dickie? If I was in the market for a babe, I'd want one a whole lot younger'n her."

"Beggars can't be choosers, Dad," Richard mumbled.

"I'll be damned," Elwood said. "You stay in bed, Dickie. I'm gonna go shave."

Chapter Nine

"You can't imagine how delighted I am to have you joining us this evening, Mr. Fundy," said Miss Grace around a warm smile. She maneuvered her charcoal gray Peugeot into a parking space at Hiram Park Elementary School. "Well, we're here, and I just know this will interest you." She leaned toward him and in a conspiratorial whisper said, "We've arranged to have a blues singer from Mississippi visit us this evening."

"I'll be damned," said Elwood.

"Oh dear, I should hope not," Miss Grace said. "My group of ladies is so looking forward to this, and we just know our musical horizons will be broadened, dare I say, enormously."

"Enormously," Elwood repeated, elongating the vowels. He got out and opened Miss Grace's door, extending his hand which she took. He leaned back and hoisted her up.

"Oh my, it's been years since someone has lifted me like that." She smoothed the front of her coat with her hands and adjusted her hat. "This is a unique gathering, Mr. Fundy. I hope there will be other men present. But our ladies are—um—somewhat elderly citizens, and many are in the Wednesday Book Club, the Symphony Auxiliary, and of course, our local Garden Club. Our common interest is music though, and that's more or less my bailiwick."

Elwood nodded, and followed her into the gymnasium annex, where a large urn of fresh-brewed coffee dominated the card table stationed just inside the annex doorway, framed by two platters of home-baked banana-carob chip cookies. Elwood grabbed two, and Miss Grace, watching, forced a tight smile. "Yes, please help yourself, Mr. Fundy. Take as many as you like."

"Chocolate's kinda thin flavored," he said, tasting one. "But they ain't half-bad." He grabbed a third cookie. "Hey, you want coffee?"

Miss Grace shook her head. "No thank you. Not just yet." She smiled as her friend, Flora Loeventhal, dropped two lumps of sugar into a china cup of coffee and handed it to a slump-shouldered, white-haired black man standing behind her.

"Marvella, allow me to present the legendary Delta blues musician, Honey Do Brooks. Mr. Brooks, Marvella Grace is in charge of this evening's program and will introduce you to our ladies and their guests."

"Howdy," said the musician, accepting his coffee, then turning to chat with another woman who was asking him about a lick she'd heard on one of his 1940s recordings she'd borrowed from the library.

Other women, hefting acoustic guitars, clustered around Mr. Brooks, one of them stretching her stubby pink fingers across frets, attempting a B-flat fifth chord Brooks had earlier demonstrated in the corridor.

Elwood, wearing a puzzled frown, looked on. "You a guitar player?" he asked the woman who seemed to be about 70.

"Well, I certainly hope to be one day, sir. I have every intention of learning a great deal from Mr. Brooks tonight."

Miss Grace smiled, and escorted Elwood to a seat next to another old gentleman who appeared to be snoozing, his chin resting on his chest.

Then she stepped to the front of the room and announced, "All right ladies, time to get down! Oh, I find it quite liberating to say 'get down.' And as I've often said, music permits each and every one of us to plumb the depths of our souls."

Honey Do Brooks pulled up a folding chair, sat, and straddled his guitar.

Miss Grace beamed at the more than two dozen women taking their seats in the annex before addressing them. "Now ladies, and guests, it gives me great pleasure to present our most distinguished guest, Mr. Honey Do Brooks."

Brooks waved at the gathering seated before him.

Miss Grace smiled at Brooks, then continued her introduction. "Mr. Brooks was born and raised in Biloxi, and has written more than 300 blues songs over a career spanning 52 years. He's made several recordings, and despite his advancing age still manages to perform at many blues clubs and other venues like this one. Without further ado, let's extend a hearty welcome to Mr. Honey Do Brooks."

Elwood joined the ladies in applause; Honey Do drained the coffee, then picked up his guitar. He began playing a raggedy

number, plucking one string at a time. His eyes closed, his head bobbed, and finally his voice emerged, raw and grainy, quiet at first, then building slowly as he sang:
"Ain't got no money,
Ain't got no home.
Ain't got no nothin'
I can call my own.
Life full of misery and pain
Goin' carry these hungry
Blues on ol' railroad train. . ."

At the conclusion of the number the ladies applauded, and Elwood inserted two fingers in his mouth and whistled, startling the man next to him. His head snapped upward and he gasped.

Honey Do nodded, acknowledging his reception. "Thank y'all so much," he mumbled softly. He sniffed, his face tilting upward. "Do I smell somethin' kinda funny, or what?"

Miss Grace crimsoned. "Oh, my, Mr. Brooks, I'm afraid the wind is wrong this evening, and we're catching the fragrance from our local paper mills."

Honey Do nodded. "Tha's good. For a minute there I thought maybe I had me an accident." He chuckled, and Miss Grace, still blushing, brought her hand to her mouth.

"Lady here, gimme cup of coffee," Honey Do continued, "but a blues man like a bit of whiskey in his java. But I don't suppose they be keeping no jar of that here." He sighed as the audience greeted his remark with subdued laughter.

He peered at them over the top of half-glasses. "Well, just exactly what is it you all's brung ol' Honey Do up here for?" He looked at Miss Grace.

"We'd like you to teach us the blues, Mr. Brooks," she said, smiling brightly. "I am schooled in the classics myself, but am little familiar with indigenous work such as you practice."

"Don' practice that much no more," Honey Do said. "I got ever'thin' right here." He tapped his forehead with a finger.

"As I told you on the phone last month, we are a group of women with broad cultural interests, but with little knowledge of the blues. We'd like to better understand them, and perhaps even attempt to write our own blues music. We may not seem like your typical blues crowd, Mr. Brooks, but I assure you our interests are catholic."

"That cool," said Honey Do. "I be an ol' Baptist, myself. All my people be stomp-down Baptist."

Miss Grace turned away from Honey Do, smiling and arching an eyebrow. "As I was about to say, many of our ladies have taken guitar lessons in anticipation of your visit, and some of us have even started to develop, shall we say—*chops*—on the harmonica—er—blues harp."

Honey Do fingered a B7 chord, strummed it, and slid up a fret and back. He smiled a gummy, toothless smile.

"Get down, Honey Do! Get down!" called a matron in the front row.

"Ma'am, ol' Honey Do's always down. That's where the blues comes from. Bein' down. You be up, you ain't gonna do no blues." He cranked on a couple of tuning pegs. "Tell y'all what we gonna do. You ladies tell ol' Honey Do what you gets the blues from. What gets you down in the dumps, so's you feel like you's 'bout done in. I never did play for no buncha ol' white ladies before, so I don' know."

One of the women in the second row stood. She removed her hat and handed it to the woman seated next to her. "Before we get down to business, I have a question," she said, smiling. "Would you mind telling us how you came by the name Honey Do? I bet this isn't the name your mother gave you when you were born."

"No. It ain't. But I been Honey Do most ever since I remember. I be the youngest of 'leven children. Momma always sayin', 'Honey, do this for me, all right baby? Honey, do that.' Pretty soon, ever'body callin' me Honey Do. Anyway, Honey Do ain't so bad. Back home, ever' time a baby come along, why Grandaddy get out the Bible and run his finger down a page 'till he come to a name. Whatever that name is, why they give it to the baby. So that's how I come to be named Segub. You can look it up. First Chronicles, second chapter, verse 21. 'An' afterward Hezron went in to the daughter of Machir the father of Gilead, who he married when he was threescore year old' an' she bare him Segub.' I be Segub too, 'cept you ain't never gonna call a young'un no name like Segub. Even Grandaddy called me Honey Do."

"I'll be damned," Elwood said. "I shoulda called Dickie Segub. Old Segub Fundy." He chuckled. Miss Grace pursed her lips and stared at him. He shrugged.

"That tune you played a few moments ago was excellent," said a woman wearing a lavender pants suit with a Hohner blues harp poking out of her breast pocket. "I'm sure all of us here can appreciate it. But it doesn't exactly speak to our experiences as older white women. Or white men," she added, indicating Elwood and the somnolent fellow next to him.

"You ain't never been hungry, that it?" Honey Do said.

"Well, hardly. In fact, judging by the way some of us look, it's just the opposite." She chuckled.

"Shoot—you don' have to be hungry to get the blues. The blues is how you feelin'. Lemme tell you a Charley Parker story. You cats know Bird? Now Bird, he had the blues real bad. But he was a wise man, and one time somebody asked how he made his music, and he said, if you don' live it it don' come out of your horn. Horn, guitar, piano, don' make no difference. See, I been hungry in my life, an' I can play about it an' sing about it. Same thing with you ladies." Then Honey Do started playing, "I Got A Woman Mean As She Can Be."

He stopped after six bars. "Y'all got a man mean as he can be?"

"That's a little out of our element too," Flora Loeventhal said. "Though a few of us might think we got a man dumb as he can be." The ladies laughed. Elwood hissed, and the woman seated behind him tapped his shoulder. "She doesn't mean you, I'm sure," she said.

Another woman in a gray bouffant and large jade earrings stood. "One day last week my daughter was having difficulty with her son's nanny. The nanny wanted a day off to register for some classes at the community college. Clara—that's my daughter—said no. Aaron had the flu and needed someone with him. Anyway, I thought I'd try that as a blues number. She picked up her Epiphone guitar, strummed a C chord *arpeggio*, cleared her throat, and sang:

"My girl, Clara got a nanny for her little boy.
Nanny for her little boy, uh-huh,
Nanny for her little boy, ooo-ooo."

She stopped. "That's as far as I've gotten. What do you think?"

After a pause, Honey Do summoned a smile and said, "That be all right. I can dig it." Honey do nodded, then lowered his voice. "What make you ladies cry?" he gently solicited.

"It's interesting you should ask that, Mr. Honey Do," said a seventyish woman in a navy suit. "When I was a little girl, my father used to go around the house singing 'Go Tell Aunt Rhody,' and every time he got to the part about the goslings crying because their mother died, why I'd just sob myself, because I knew how I'd feel if my mother had died." She smiled. "Is 'Go Tell Aunt Rhody' a blues song?"

"Lordy," said Honey Do, rolling his eyes. "Wonder what ol' B. B. King say about this?"

Another woman said something about how terribly animals are treated these days, and that this inhumanity is enough to give any sensitive soul the blues. Several women applauded the remark.

Elwood nudged the man next to him, shook his head, but said nothing. The other man opened his eyes, then closed them again.

"Lordy," Honey Do said again. "Well, I know you ladies dig food, so how 'bout 'Gimme a Pig Foot and a Bottle of Beer?'"

"I'm sorry, we can't have beer in the school either," said Miss

Grace. "But I should have inquired as to what you might like for a snack." She smiled apologetically. "We don't have pigs' feet. Only coffee and cookies."

"Lady, that's a song. Doctor tells ol' Honey Do, go easy on the salt these days. Got me high blood pressure, so I don' be eatin' no pig feet. I *sing* 'em." He paused and shrugged then looked at Miss Grace. "I don' know 'bout this. But hey, let's try somethin' different. Ain't none of you ladies been lonesome? I be talkin' 'bout that mean lonesome. The lonesome-ist you ever been, and how you so sick from that lonesome that you could just cry. You oughta listen to ol' John Lee Hooker. There's a dude what knows lonesome."

Flora stood again. "I don't think lonesome applies much to us either. I mean, when my husband, Clarence is away on business, I have so many friends that I can call, and right away I'm cheered up. If you've got good friends, I don't see why anyone would ever be lonesome."

"None of your men done up an' leave you?" Honey Do asked.

"He'd better not," one woman asserted. Others chuckled.

"Ladies, what give you pain?" Honey Do asked hopefully. "Blues come from pain. 'Course there's what they call the happy blues too, and that may be what y'all got."

Miss Grace, who'd been standing near the coffee urn, strode forward and stood near Honey Do. "What you say is unfortunately true, Mr. Brooks. Sadly, we are an altogether happy lot, are we not?" She faced the audience. "Whence cometh our pain? What I'm hearing tonight is that our so-called blues experiences are not from the deep well of tradition, with which Mr. Brooks is so very familiar. But, in the fullness of time, things change. I suspect that's true even of the blues Mr. Brooks so ably performs.

"Perhaps the best thing we could do right now is have Mr. Brooks further enlighten us with a few of his favorite blues numbers, and then there will be time for more coffee and cookies. I'm sure our guest will avail himself to any of us who might want to try writing her own blues song, like Charlene."

"Lordy," said Honey Do, shaking his head. "You ladies is somethin' else." He retuned his guitar and ran through a medley of songs by Howlin' Wolf, Mississippi Fred McDowell, Robert Johnson, and Bessie Smith, before Miss Grace put her hand on his shoulder.

"This has been wonderful," she said. "You have enriched us beyond measure, Mr. Brooks. I know we'll be talking about your visit here for many years to come. Now, I'm sure there are those of you who'd like to chat with Mr. Brooks, so while I fetch him another cup of coffee, you get some yourselves. Also, a big thank you to Dagney Sloan, who made the delicious cookies."

Honey Do moaned, and motioned to Miss Grace, who leaned in as he mumbled, "You sure there's no whiskey nowhere 'round here, lady? I'm parched."

"I'm with you, pal," said Elwood, who had overheard the remark.

Miss Grace grimaced, forced a smile and apologized to Honey Do, as two women approached the aging blues master, one suggesting a song theme. "I have seven granddaughters and each of them expects me to buy all my Girl Scout cookies from her."

The other woman thought Title IX equity for female college athletes could work well as a blues song.

Miss Grace, sipping black coffee, approached Elwood. "Wasn't this edifying, Mr. Fundy? I'm just thrilled we've had this opportunity."

"It wasn't bad, I guess," said Elwood. "But between you and me, I'm a big fan of country music. Far as I'm concerned you can't beat ol' Willie Nelson or that gal with the big bazooms, Dolly Parton."

"Mr. Fundy, really."

"Well, maybe they ain't real. You see her on television, and who's to know?"

Miss Grace turned away, embarrassed. She moved to the coffee table and tried lifting the urn, but Elwood took it. "Where to, Gracie?"

"Why thank you, Mr. Fundy." She pointed to the kitchen door and he nodded. "Right-o."

Twenty minutes later, after most of the blues ladies had departed, Miss Grace finished tidying up the kitchen, and Elwood tried conversing with the man who'd slept through most of the presentation. But the fellow was only interested in grousing about his wife who'd stayed behind to get help with a piece she'd been writing.

Honey Do was still seated at the front of the room. He was plucking his guitar, mouth agape and eyes vacant. The woman beamed as the ancient blues man growled through her lyrics:

"I always dead-head my petunias, yeah.
Dagney and Phyllis cut their back.
My 'tunias won the blue ribbon, uh-huh, uh-huh.
Now Dagney and Phyllis got the dead-head
Pee-tunia blues. Dead-head pee-tunia blues. Yeah."

Chapter Ten

When Richard arrived at Button Gwinnet Senior High School on Monday morning, Hulot Piquete was standing in front of Richard's classroom, his arms folded across his chest. The corners of his mouth were pulled downward. He was shaking his head. "Come along, Fundy," he said curtly, and with a sweep of his head, beckoned Richard follow him to his own office, closing the door as soon as Richard entered.

"I'll be blunt and to the point." He snapped open a folded sheet of paper. "'Mr. Richard Fundy is hereby suspended from teaching duties effective immediately until further notice for conduct unbecoming a teacher in Independent School District 302A.' This letter of notification is signed by the superintendent, Dr. Clovelink, and by myself, of course." He thrust it toward Richard. "Take it, Fundy. This is your copy."

Richard sighed audibly, then coughed and cleared his throat. "What is the charge?" His voice croaked hoarsely. His temples pounded.

"Charge? Make that plural, Fundy. Charges. Disturbing the peace, disrupting that wedding. Brawling, I shouldn't doubt. Your face is a fright, Fundy. And then this disgusting exhibition of—what do they call it? Ferret-legging? I can't imagine what you were thinking. And in that Waltzing Walleye denizen of lower life forms, of all places. Making matters the worse, it's all in this morning's *Pine-Journal*. And look, here's your picture in the Lifestyle section in the Duluth Sunday newspaper. 'Area Teacher Wins Ferret-Legging Competion in Cloquet.' What have I said about teachers frequenting saloons, Fundy? It places us in compromising situations. I tend to look the other way as educators are entitled to a little libation now and then, so long as they don't compromise themselves or their profession. But here you are, Fundy, big as you please, engaging in a rather ribald competition with common riff-raff. I'm told the event will be on one of the cable channels too, for everybody in Carlton and St. Louis Counties to see. Oh, the shame of it. It'll be a real challenge to overcome this negative publicity you've wreaked upon us. And if that weren't enough, here you are again, same paper, but in the police report this time. You and that father of yours, Fundy, it boggles the mind. You had to know all this would catch up with you. Did you think the board office could be hoodwinked? Did you hold your principal in so little regard that you thought he'd never learn of this? I do read the papers, and so does our superintendent." Dr. Piquete dabbed at his lips with a handkerchief, then inserted it in his pocket again.

"You're caught in a steamroller here, Fundy," he continued, "and it makes your position here hardly tenable. I had hopes for you, truly I did. I saw in you an inexperienced teacher, to be sure, but at the same time, I saw a man with certain qualities—maturity, a proclivity toward scholarship, which sadly, we don't often find in K through 12 education anymore. I saw that in you, Fundy, but I was obviously mistaken. You've made transgressions that even the rankest of beginners wouldn't consider in their wildest imaginings. I know I'll never understand it. But that's how things are right now. You must leave school immediately, and not return until after your hearing. I will accompany you back to your room while you gather personal effects. Other than that, I'm afraid you're not to set foot inside this building, nor anyplace on this campus. That includes the parking lot and the football stadium as well. I trust I—that is, the board and I—have made ourselves quite clear on this matter."

Richard stared at his shoes, blinked back tears, then straightened and nodded at his principal.

As they headed down the hall, Dr. Piquete marching several steps ahead of Richard, the principal stopped suddenly and turned around. "I have a need to know, Fundy. Can you explain what impelled you toward this bizarre behavior? And I hope you won't fall back on that shopworn 'lack of succor' notion you fostered earlier."

"It doesn't matter."

"Suit yourself," said Dr. Piquete curtly, and he unlocked the classroom door and followed Richard as the teacher gathered personal items from his desk and a cabinet. "I shouldn't think it necessary to personally escort you to the parking lot. I will merely ask for your key and request that you depart immediately. Do not engage in conversation with staff or students." He sighed. "This entire affair is totally regrettable, I'm sad to say."

"Thank you," Richard said because he could think of nothing else.

Loaded with briefcase and files, Richard made his way toward the parking lot exit, but was intercepted by Miss Grace. "I'll not chide you, Mr. Fundy, if that's what you're thinking. Not for one minute. I understand what stress can do to a person, and force the mind to play tricks. There have been times, Mr. Fundy, when I myself have heard voices inaccessible to others. Angelic voices singing their hearts out, Mr. Fundy, and naturally, being a singer myself, I would join them. Have you heard voices? Oh, you needn't answer. It would embarrass you. But I do understand what you're going through just now and I'd like to think that you could call on me—"

"Thank you, Miss Grace," Richard interrupted. "I appreciate your concern, and in days to come I'll no doubt engage in much soul plumbing. But I've been ordered off the premises. You'll have to excuse me."

"I had a nice little visit with your father the other night. I was so very pleased he could join us in our celebration of the blues. Has he spoken of it to you, Richard? I do hope he has. What a charming man he is. Please tell him I found him so, won't you? Oh, say you will, Mr. Fundy. Such a very charming gentleman. One so rarely encounters such a man these days."

Without glancing at the music teacher, Richard said, "I'll tell him," then continued toward the exit, aware that Miss Grace would be staring after him until he was gone.

Outside, the air had freshened; a hint of sun had broken through the fog, a hopeful sign that might have, on other days, lessened Richard's melancholia. But he paid no mind to the weather, nor atmospheric conditions, and drove immediately to Luther's house.

Johann Strauss the Younger, chained to a large tree, began leaping and barking, announcing his arrival. Speaking softly to the animal, Richard approached, but the dog, in a state of excited agitation sniffed, circled, raised a leg and whizzed, splattering Richard's shoes.

He was wiping them with his handkerchief when Luther appeared on the front stoop. "Rich—what's up? Why aren't you in school?"

Richard held the handkerchief in his hand, looking for some place to deposit it. Finding nothing, he sighed and jammed it into his coat pocket. He walked toward Luther as Johann resumed yapping. "I'm suspended, Luther."

"What for? Ferret-legging?" Luther jumped down off the stoop and jogged toward Richard.

"In part, yes. Ferret-legging, disturbing the peace, cooning apples." Richard moaned and leaned against a birch tree. "It's Dad's fault. He's gone off the deep end and taken me with him. I'm ruined, finished. If I had any confidence at all, I'd strangle myself with my tie."

"Geez, Rich." Luther put his hand on Richard's shoulder. "Come on in. You look awful."

"I should hope so," Richard said weakly.

He sunk into Luther's worn sofa, loosened his tie and unfastened his top shirt button. "Any suggestions, Luther?"

"Tea? Coffee? Something stronger?"

"Whatever's handy."

Luther brought coffee in a mug bearing the logo of the Savannah Woodwind Octet, and handed it to Richard. "So, what happened today?"

Richard cradled the cup in his hands and told Luther how he'd been met by Piquete and given the letter of suspension. He would get a hearing, but wasn't at all sure he had the heart to fight for the job.

"I think it's winnable, Rich." Luther sipped coffee. "They can't make this stick. I mean, nothing you were involved with had anything to do with your job. You're bound to be reinstated."

Richard shrugged. "I'm not sure of that. This isn't a large district, Luther. You can't expect to teach school when practically everyone knows about the baggage you're carrying. So I'm reinstated. Everybody points at you as that weird guy with ferrets in his pants, or the crazy teacher who steals apples, fights at weddings, the whole nine yards."

"Except for the ferret-legging, none of the other stuff was really you."

Richard snorted a derisive laugh. "Who knows that, Luther? You and I and, for what it's worth, Dad. What good does that do? Perception is reality, and I'd never overcome that." He glanced at his untouched coffee, tasted it and shuddered.

"What're you gonna tell your dad?"

"The truth—that thanks to him I'm *persona non grata* in this county."

"You want me to go with you, Rich?"

A thin smile played over Richard's lips. "Thanks, no, Luther. I hate to take you away from your work."

"Hey, it's no bother."

Richard thanked him again, but said it was a family matter, and that he'd call and let Luther know how it went. He finished his coffee while Luther ran a few *arpeggios* on the piano, adding to the score he was composing. It sounded to Richard rather like the notes were warring against each other in a quest to dominate, to be heard. Richard stood, tapped Luther's shoulder and indicated he was leaving.

Still in robe and pajamas, Elwood was lying on the couch watching a morning game show on television when Richard entered. Elwood propped himself on his elbow. "Been expectin' you, Dickie."

"How can that be? It's Monday, and I'm supposed to be in school."

"On the radio, Dickie. News report about you, and that you been suspended from teaching. I always had a funny feeling that something like this was gonna happen to you, and now it did." Elwood sighed, and drew himself into a seated position. "I know you're feeling pretty down, Dickie, and I'm real sorry about that. But who says life is fair? It ain't, and that's that.

"Now you take me, for instance. Hell, Dickie, come down to it, you don't know hardly nothing about me. Or the things that happened to me, things I had to deal with. And I never expected you to. But you might have tried to understand that, like Dr. Incapace's been sayin', I'm a conflicted man."

Richard groaned and nodded. "I don't know what I'm going to do, Dad. My whole life is coming apart at the seams."

Elwood looked up at Richard and coughed a soft, bubbly cough. "That's what I been tryin' to tell you for years, Dickie." Elwood stood. "One thing I believe is it ain't right to kick a man when he's down in the dumps. But on the other hand, when a fella's down as much as you he can't go no farther anyway. So it probably don't make all that much difference, except to me, of course. This thing's been bottled up inside me for a long time, and Dr. Incapace says I got to get it out. And I want to get it out, Dickie, before I die."

"Whatever, Dad," Richard said, without looking at Elwood.

"This ain't gonna be easy for either of us, Dickie. Dr. Incapace says it's a demon that's burdened me practically my whole adult life." Elwood paced in small circles. "So, here goes. Now pay close attention, Dickie."

Richard sighed. "Sure, Dad." He propped a pillow behind his head and closed his eyes. "Go ahead. I'm listening. Wait, wait. As I was leaving school this morning, Miss Grace wanted me to be sure and tell you she found you to be very charming."

"The hell," Elwood said, then cleared his throat and swallowed. "And you say she's hot for me. I never thought a woman that old could be hot for anything. When they're post-menopausal, Dickie, women don't get heated up no more. I really don't think old Gracie is no different."

Richard exhaled audibly, his eyes still closed.

"You'd listen better with your eyes open, Dickie, but what the hell." Elwood stepped to the mantel and picked up the old wedding photo of himself—an army PFC— and Richard's mother. He jabbed a finger at his wife. "Your mother had some good qualities, Dickie. I want to say that right off. It ain't right to speak ill of the dead. But let me ask you this, ever in your whole life did anyone ever say you looked like me?"

Eyes still closed, Richard said, "I don't know, probably. Now that you mention it, though, most of the time people thought I resembled Mom."

"That's right, Dickie. You always resembled your mother. Never once did anyone ever say to me that you resembled your old man. But..." Elwood paused and returned the photo to the mantel. "But on the other hand, maybe you do resemble your father, Dickie. Could be, I suppose."

Richard sat up, rubbing his eyes. "Dad, what are you saying?"

Elwood shook his head and gazed at the wedding photo. "It's a funny story, Dickie, but you gotta know the truth."

"Dad, what's going on? You've been paying too much attention to that Incapace jerk."

"He ain't a jerk, Dickie. And I don't want to hear no more about that. Now, you listen, Dickie, because I made up my mind to tell you everything, and it ain't no bed of roses for me. You don't remember none of this, but back when your mother and I got married, I was in the army. Not long afterward, they shipped me to Thule, Greenland, a godforsaken hellhole, Dickie. Had to spend 12 months up there half freezin' to death. But back then a soldier couldn't take his family with him. Had to go it alone. So anyway, I may not have been the best soldier, but I did my duty, and off I go to Thule."

Elwood paused to light a cigarette, tossing the spent match into the fireplace. "It wasn't no fun, but I made it. There were some fellas went stir crazy up there, but not me. So anyway, about a month before I was supposed to come back home, I get a letter from your mother telling me there's a little surprise for me when I get back. And when I come back, the surprise turns out to be you, Dickie"

"Dad."

Elwood held up his hand. "Don't interrupt me, Dickie. You were the surprise. Well, what am I supposed to think of that? So anyway, your mother sits me down and explains herself. First, you gotta understand that your mother's maternal grandmother on her mother's side was Eyetalian. She was an immigrant from the south, some place your mother always called Calabria, I think it was. Anyway, this old grandma used to tell your mother stories about magical stuff, I guess, and your mother maybe believed it, because this is what she tells me.

"Couple months after I shipped out, she was missin' me terrible, she says. Just awful, couldn't hardly bear it. So one night, she tells me she has this dream, and I'm there with her in the bed. She said the dream was so strong that it had to be real. Don't ask me how, Dickie, but she says it happens all the time with Eyetalians. Dr. Incapace, who is also of Eyetalian extraction, told me that lotsa times when Eyetalian men went off to wars, which they mostly lost, they'd come back and find new babies in the cribs or on the way. And everybody thought those babies was made in dreams too. Hell, what did I know? So it was in that dream that you was conceived, according to your mother. Well, I'm a young man, and I'd heard some of the old grandma's stories before, and I wanted to believe your mother. 'Course, I don't remember nothing about no dream like that. Wasn't my dream, though, was it? I was up in Greenland, freezin' my balls.

"I know I ain't the smartest man ever lived, Dickie, but then again, I ain't the dumbest either. I always been suspicious about it, but never said nothin'. I mean, you come back and find your wife with a baby boy, a couple months old—. Anyway, I had this on my mind off and on all these years, Dickie. You grew up and you wasn't nothin' like me, at all. I sorta suspected something, but I tried putting it out of my mind. Hadn't a been for Dr. Incapace, why who knows how long I'd have kept trying to keep it out of my mind, which isn't healthy. Dr. Incapace flat out says them dreams were a buncha malarkey. He says, 'Elwood, for your own sanity and well-being, I haveta say that dream conceptions, despite the traditions of Eyetalian fairy tales, are impossible. Never happened. The sooner you come to grips with that, the better off you'll be, and you'll have resolved one of the major issues in your life.'" Elwood paused and sighed. "So in the end, I was cuckooed by your mother, Dickie." He cleared his throat.

"You gotta resolve the issues in your life. And I say this from experience. I got this bum ticker, and I betcha it comes from tryin' to keep this dream of your mother's outta my mind, but not bein' able to." He coughed and blew his nose. "Anyway, there it is. Now you know. I'm real sorry about it too. So I get my big issue resolved before I die, but you, poor little sucker, you got a bunch of 'em now yourself. Take my advice, Dickie, don't let 'em go unresolved as long as I did. It ain't healthy."

"Dad."

"No, Dickie," Elwood said softly, turning away. "I ain't your dad."

Chapter Eleven

Richard sat on the sofa, shielding his eyes with his hands. His breathing came in shallow, aspirate gasps. Elwood, not looking at Richard, propped himself against the mantel, smoke from the cigarette between his fingers curling above his head. He coughed a phlegmy cough. "So, anyway, Dickie, as luck would have it, you and me ain't even related to each other. Kinda hard to accept, even for me, after all these years of knowin' each other, and livin' together." Elwood pursed his lips and scratched his chest.

Without looking up, Richard whispered hoarsely, "Dad, are you sure? I mean, I've never heard—"

"Dickie, I haveta go on what Dr. Incapace says, and of course, my gut feeling, which I've had all these years. Come right down to it, Dickie, put yourself in my shoes here. I'm an old coot who never fathered any children. A man likes to think he's left somebody to carry on the name, you know? And in my case it won't be long before they ring my bell. Even if I did go out and find some younger woman to have my child, I wouldn't be around to watch him grow up, like I did with you, Dickie. It wouldn't be the same, bein' dead and leavin' a young kid to grow up without a daddy. Oh, I suppose you could watch out for him, Dickie, but that would be just another burden for you to carry. And from what I've seen, you ain't all that big on carryin' burdens." Elwood snuffed his cigarette and turned toward Richard. "But I gotta say this, I feel a whole lot better gettin' this off my chest. And if it hadn't been for Dr. Incapace, it'd never a happened."

Richard exhaled. "Dad, there's one way to prove this, you know. We could have blood tests. DNA tests, which would—"

Elwood shook his head as he interrupted. "You don't get it,

Dickie. I wasn't even here when you was made. As near as I can figure I wasn't even in the picture. I was thousands a miles away up in Greenland."

Elwood balled several sheets of newspaper and placed them in the fireplace. He struck a wooden match and lit the papers, then he removed the wedding photo from the mantel and tossed it into the blaze.

Richard leaped up. "Dad! Don't. What are you doing?" He rushed to the fireplace in an attempt to retrieve the photo but Elwood blocked him, and the picture melted in a hiss of blue-orange flames.

"Dad," Richard said softly as his shoulders sagged.

"So that's that, Dickie. You enter this world with nothin', and far as I'm concerned, you leave it the same way. It's like I was never married to that woman at all," he said, and turned around to slowly mount the stairs to his bedroom.

"Dad, wait." Richard started after Elwood. "I mean—I mean—what does this mean?"

Elwood turned around. "To be plain about it, Dickie, it means some other man is your father." Elwood entered his room and closed the door.

Richard trudged downstairs and slumped in the sofa, emitting soft groans for several moments, before reaching for the phone. He dialed Luther's number.

Luther offered to come right over, but Richard said it would probably do him more good to get out of the house, and would Luther mind if he came over again?

"Absolutely, come on. I'll rustle up something for lunch. Omelets sound okay?"

"Fine, but I'm not sure I could eat anything, Luther. I'm a total wreck."

The closet door creaked when he opened it to grab a jacket, and Elwood hollered down to him. "Dickie, come up here a minute, will you?"

Richard went to Elwood's room. Elwood was lying on the bed, his eyes closed. "I don't want you to think I don't care about your feelings, Dickie. I do. It's been a real hard day for both of us. But fact is, you and I have been close. You might say, like father and son."

"I know, Dad."

Elwood opened one eye. "I've been like a dad to you, anyway. And you've been like a son to me. Fact is, you're all I have, sort of. And just because things have turned out funny like this, I'd like to think I could still count on you to take care of things like I said after I'm gone." He sat up and clutched Richard's wrists.

"Yeah. Sure." Richard released Elwood's grip and backed out

of the door as he closed it.

"Garth Brooks' Greatest Hits" was on in Luther's living room when Richard arrived. Johann Strauss the Younger did not bark, though he did amble over to sniff Richard's shoes and cast an expectant glance for an ear-scratching.

Luther hollered from the kitchen that he was out of eggs, and was making some Chinese pepper steak instead. "Didn't have any beef either, Rich," he called. "But last week a few of the rez boys gave me some venison. That'll work just as well."

"Whatever," Richard said, pointedly ignoring Johann, who whimpered once, then plopped down in front of the rocking chair with a thump.

Luther, wearing a chef's apron, entered, wiping his hands on a towel. "I know it's kind of early, but you want a beer or something?"

"Nothing, Luther, thanks. I don't know what I want, what I think anymore. I'm just totally messed up."

"Yeah, I gathered that. Listen, tell me the whole story. Is Elwood all right?"

Richard nodded. "I guess so. This is really a shock, Luther. I don't know whether to believe him or not. I mean, we've always had this strange relationship anyway. My gut instinct is—I don't know what my gut instinct is, Luther. I'm not sure I know anything anymore."

"You could put this to rest with a simple blood test, Rich. Elwood's a strange guy. Maybe it's just his age."

Richard nodded. "He's got this preoccupation with death. Has had it ever since I moved back, actually. That's why I'm inclined to believe him. He wants to clean the slate." Richard chuckled without humor. "Pretty fantastic story, actually," he said, and told Luther about the myth of Calabrian dreams and how his mother halfway convinced Elwood of this alleged immaculate conception. When he finished he said, "I never detected anything odd about my mother, Luther. It was Dad who was, as you put it, strange. Geez, I don't think I can ever call him anything but Dad."

"I know what you mean, buddy." Luther bent down and scratched Johann's ears.

"In the final analysis, living around here will be impossible for me, Luther. I'll have to start over someplace else, and it's not likely I can get a teaching job again."

Luther argued that the battle wasn't lost yet, and that Richard should stay on and fight for his present position, which he would probably retain. "Forget about opprobrium," Luther said. "In a few weeks it's all water under the bridge."

"It's more than that, Luther. There will always be something with Dad, and I can't avoid getting dragged into his affairs. I can't live that way."

"Take a few days to think things over," Luther said. "You need to get away, stay here. I've got an extra room you can use as long as you like."

Richard brightened. "Thanks. I will. I'll go home and pack a few things and be back in an hour."

Elwood was sitting in the recliner, the television tuned to CNN, when Richard entered. He was wearing pajamas. "Couldn't sleep, Dickie," he said absently. "Feelin' awful restless."

"Don't bother yourself, Dad," Richard said. "I'm just going to grab a few things and stay with Luther for a while until I sort things out."

"Probably a good idea. It's meant a world of difference to me to get things sorted out, and in the end it'll be good for you too. That's life, hey?"

Richard went to his room and threw clothing into a small suitcase, then went back downstairs.

Elwood still sat in the recliner. "Dickie, maybe we should have this one more little talk before you go."

"About what?"

"Stuff. I ain't too good with words, Dickie. While you was gone, old Miss Grace called from school to see how you were. Between you and me and the fence post, I think she probably wanted to talk to me. She's probably a nice old gal, Dickie, but I'd appreciate it if you'd tell her she ain't my type. Know what I mean?"

"Not really. I hardly ever knew what you meant. And it isn't likely I'm going to be seeing her any time soon. You're on your own with that one, Dad." Richard looked down at Elwood. "Anything else you wanted to talk about?"

"Your father."

"Look, I don't think I can take anymore trauma. Can't it wait, Dad?" He started for the door, but Elwood reached out and grabbed his sleeve.

"You forget already? I ain't your dad."

"Oh, sorry." He eased away from Elwood.

"But I'm pretty sure I know who is."

Richard groaned. He dropped the suitcase and sat on the sofa. "All right, shoot me."

"What's that supposed to mean? Shoot me? I'm tryin' to help you here. I'd never shoot you, Dickie."

"I know, I know. Sorry, Dad."

Elwood eyed Richard, then cleared his throat. "I don't imagine you're gonna like this any, but like Dr. Incapace says, 'the truth is strong medicine.' Dickie, as you know, your mother was very involved with that there Unitarian church that later become the Free Huey Newton Universalist Society. Maybe too involved for her own good. That's probably why I never was much of a churchgoer myself. Don't get me wrong, Dickie. There's fine people who used to go up there, but some folks go over the edge, if you know what I mean." He looked at Richard, who acknowledged with an impatient nod.

"She spent an awful lot of time at the church even before we was married, and she used to write to me about how much help and encouragement she got from the minister there." He paused again and stared at Richard.

"Okay, go on," Richard said.

"I'm pretty sure he gave her more than encouragement, Dickie. I think he gave her you. You're a preacher's kid, Dickie. What do you think of that?"

Richard inhaled and exhaled loudly. He wiped his lips on a handkerchief. "Who is this guy, Dad?"

Elwood rose up on his tiptoes. "Reverend Durfee, Dickie."

❖❖❖❖❖

Before leaving the house on Mister Lane, Richard was beset with diarrhea, and Elwood made him a pot of tea. "About the best thing for the trots, Dickie. That's one thing I learned from your mother. Tea for the trots."

After drinking half a cup, Richard headed back to Luther's home, arriving as Luther was putting a skillet of pepper steak on the kitchen table. He had set a stoneware plate at either end of the table. "I held chow, Rich," he said. "Take just a minute to reheat in the microwave."

"I'm not hungry, Luther. Stomach's kinda loose. And maybe in a minute you won't feel like eating either." He unfastened the top three buttons on his shirt. "Geez, Luther, I don't know where to begin, or how to tell you this. But unless Dad's gone way over the edge, he thinks your father is—well, my father too." Richard shook his head. "There—that's what he said, and I'm telling you, because I guess you should know, and I don't know what the hell else to say or how to say it, or if it's true, or if I'm stark raving mad myself. But there it is."

"I'll be damned," Luther said, and whistled through his teeth. At the sound of the whistle, Johann Strauss the Younger bounded toward his master, leaped on him, and leaned against him, standing on his hind legs. "Later, buddy," Luther said, and pushed the dog away.

"I mean, you just never know what kind of curves and tricks life has up its sleeve, do you?" Richard offered, shaking his head. He sat on a wooden kitchen chair. "A few days ago, I'm going along just like everybody else, then whammo."

"Whammo is right, Rich. I can't believe it."

"I'm not sure I do, Luther. These last few days have hacked the wind out of my sails. Beyond that...."

Luther had walked to the kitchen doorway and braced himself against the frame. "I think we both need to talk to your dad—to Elwood, Rich. I have a ton of questions."

"Yeah, but not right now. I need some time to take a few deep breaths, Luther. He seemed kind of shaky himself. Let's go over first thing tomorrow and maybe we can get some answers out of him. I don't know. Right now my brain is a puddle."

Luther faced him. "I can appreciate that, Rich. But now this concerns me, and I don't think I can wait until tomorrow. I have to talk to him right away." He touched Richard's shoulder. "Look, you don't want to talk now, fine. Stay here. Eat something. But I have to talk to your dad—Elwood, that is."

Richard nodded mutely. Luther grabbed an Atlanta Braves warm-up jacket and hurried outside.

The phone rang in Luther's kitchen. Richard, eyes closed, head down on the table, gas bubbling in his bowels, did not move. After the fourth ring, the answering machine picked up the call, and Richard could hear Luther's urgent cry for him to pick up the damn phone now.

"Rich, oh, God, Rich. He's dead." Luther's shout bordered on hysteria. "Your dad's dead, Rich."

Luther explained that when he arrived, Elwood didn't answer the door, but Luther could see him on the sofa. He tried the door, which was open, and went in. He couldn't rouse Elwood, and called for an ambulance. But Elwood was gone by the time they arrived, he said. "You better get over here, Rich."

Richard navigated the county roads back to Mister Lane. The ambulance and police vehicle were in the driveway behind Luther's Honda.

Richard ran to the house. An officer said, "You his son?"

"Yeah, sort of."

The officer eyed Richard for a moment. "I'm sorry, sir," he said.

"Oh God, Rich," Luther said. "This is just awful. I'm so sorry." He put his arm around Richard's shoulder, and together they looked at Elwood's lifeless form on the sofa. "I had them wait until you got here," Luther said. "I figured that'd be the right thing to do."

Richard nodded. "That's that, I guess." He looked at Elwood, then back at Luther.

Both the officer and ambulance crew stared at Richard. "Is there anything else, sir?" one of them said.

Richard shook his head.

The officer took a final look around the living room, and again expressed his sympathies, then he left with the ambulance crew who offered to drop Elwood's body at the mortuary.

"Geez, Rich," said Luther. "I mean talk about bad luck. If it weren't for bad luck you wouldn't have any luck at all. You know how terrible I feel about this."

"Yeah. Me too," Richard said, before picking up the ringing telephone. Hulot Piquete said a date had been set for Richard's hearing.

"Now isn't a good time to talk," Richard said. "My father—that is, Elwood Fundy has just passed away. I really can't discuss anything now."

Dr. Piquete stammered an apology, offered his condolences, and said he'd be right over before hanging up.

Richard stared at the receiver and moaned, "Now Hulot Piquete is coming over."

"He won't stay long," Luther said. "I'll get rid of him."

Richard and Luther sat across from each other in the Fundy front room, quietly chatting about recent events, the life of Elwood, his penchant for art and music. Luther tried cheering Richard by referring to incidents concerning Elwood that he found amusing. Richard was unmoved. Twenty minutes later, Hulot Piquete rapped at the door.

The grim-faced principal entered and removed his homburg. He extended his hand to Richard and clapped him on the back. "Terrible news, Fundy. Terrible, coming at a time like this. He was a man with more quiddities than anybody I've ever met, but yet and still, he was your father. You don't replace your father, Fundy. None of us do. This is a terrible blow." Dr. Piquete smiled at Luther and walked over to shake his hand. "Mr. Burgess-Durfee, nice to see you again, sir. Good to know you're standing by Fundy at a time like this. The man needs all the support he can get."

Luther nodded. "We're just getting started on arrangements, and have quite a bit to do, so—"

"Glory, don't I know that. I'm not here in any official capacity, Fundy, but rather as a friend, a mentor, who understands your loss at this time. And if there's anything I can do, why I hope you'll not hesitate to call. Now, when is the funeral? I speak for the entire staff at Button Gwinnet when I say that whatever our differences, we put them behind us at a time like this and get behind our own."

"Mr. Fundy wasn't a religious man," Richard said. "He'd probably prefer a gathering of his friends at Art's Place. I haven't made arrangements yet, but you'll see a notice in the paper."

"Oh, well, to each his own, I suppose. I, for one, certainly would hope to attend, if time away from the office can be managed. Please know that, Fundy." He looked around the living room, wrinkled his nose at the lingering tobacco odor. "We can discuss the matter of your hearing later in the week, or even next week, if you wish. It makes matters all the more difficult now for everyone, though. I feel awful about arranging a hearing for a teacher we're moving to dismiss, especially when that teacher has so recently become an orphan." He put his hand on Luther's arm. "I've dealt with many students over the years who became orphans while in my school, Mr. Burgess-Durfee. Dealt with reports of highway slaughters, suicides—even murder-suicides, of all things—let alone the illnesses that take a fatal turn. My heart has always gone out to those youngsters. But you know, it's no different when you're an adult orphan, is it? It marks the end of a certain passage of time, of life, and one is bereft, consumed by feelings of despair and despondency. And don't I know it." He moved his hat from hand to hand. "Well, again, my deepest sympathies to you, Fundy. I can't say for certain how your hearing will go, but I will take a moment to show my impartiality, when I say good luck to you." He returned his hat to his head, waved, and departed.

As he left, voices were heard outside the door, and the bell rang. Luther opened it and Marvella Grace stepped inside. Upon spotting Richard, she rushed to him, and embraced him, tears coursing down her cheeks. "Oh, how terribly, terribly sorry I am, Mr. Fundy. Your father, oh, what a tragedy. Words can't convey my deep sorrow. When I heard the news I couldn't face my classes. To be teaching students when a dear one has been summoned...."

"Yes, thank you, Miss Grace."

She stepped back from Richard and looked up into his face, still clutching his hands in her moist palms. "I didn't know him at all well, but I had the feeling we were soon to become fast friends. I wonder if he might have felt the same toward me."

Richard nodded. "He mentioned you on several occasions."

Miss Grace sniffled. "Oh, the dear, dear man. He had such unique qualities, Richard. Oh, I can see many of those qualities in you. His love of music and the arts. Your friendship with Mr. Burgess-Durfee here certainly supports that. Your father had characteristics I could relate to. It has been years since I felt that way about another, Richard." She dabbed her eyes with a lace hankie. "I don't know if I believe in omens, but it seemed to me your father and I were on a singular course, a pathway, don't you see. This is why I feel his loss so acutely." She blew her nose. "Though not so acutely as you, of course."

"Yes," Richard said. "It was very nice of you to stop by."

"It was the very least I could do. And such misfortune has come your way of late, Richard. I can barely stand to think about it. Speaking for myself, I trust it won't be long before you're back with us at Button Gwinnet."

"It's kind of you to say that."

Miss Grace put her hankie in her purse. "If I may, Richard, I'd be pleased and honored if you would ask me to sing something at your father's service."

Richard glanced at Luther and rolled his eyes. "I think I've got just the piece, Rich," Luther said. He stood and approached Miss Grace. "Give me your address and I'll drop off the music tomorrow."

Chapter Twelve

Art's Place was nearly packed for Elwood's memorial service. A Florsheim shoebox containing Elwood's ashes rested on a Hoskar Bunting pedestal of concrete block atop the table in Elwood's favorite booth near the ferns. A spray of roses and mums covered most of the box. On an easel adjacent to the booth rested a collage rendered in the style of Stuart Davis. Irma Novocella had created the collage, arranging large colored cardboard letters spelling ELWOOD. Smaller letters formed words that lacked association: BUBBLE, RAINGEAR, LIMELIGHT. These words were asymmetrically arranged around Elwood's name against a backdrop of bright fuschia with a black border.

At the old upright piano near the front, Luther, playing a medley of Vladimir Stcherrbatcheff nonettes arranged for piano, paused as Miss Grace took a position next to him. She looked at the box of Elwood's remains and nodded. Luther seamlessly segued into "Buffalo Gals Won't You Come Out Tonight?" as Miss Grace lifted her voice, and mourners hoisted glasses in Elwood's memory.

When the song ended, Arthur Fykes said, "Okay, let's get started with the send-off. Elwood was our friend, and while we may not all have loved the man, we were always aware of his presence." He raised his glass. "I'll miss the old boy."

Hoskar Bunting walked to Arthur and draped an arm over his shoulder. "Elwood Fundy was an odd fellow. I mean that in a good way. He understood art and what it meant to be an artist. I come along at a time when it wasn't easy for a tradesman to get accepted as an artist. It's a whole lot different today. Shoot, today every stonemason, every landscaper and lumberjack's uncle thinks he's an artist. But back in them days Elwood always used to say to me, 'Hoskar, I say you're an artist. If you say you're an artist, who's to know the difference?' That meant a lot to me and encouraged me to stick with it. Now, I'm by-God successful. If it hadn't a been for old Elwood, I don't know, maybe I'd still be sweatin' like a stuck pig puttin' in somebody's basement. So here's to ya, Elwood, old pal. I know we'll hardly ever forget you." Hoskar lifted his large, callused hand containing a can of Miller. "Down the hatch," he said, chugging the beer.

At that point Luther resumed playing. As Grieg's "In the Hall of Mountain King," ascended through the atrium, Irma Novacello said, "Elwood loved that song. It won't be the same hearing it again without him around."

Dr. Incapace rose to speak. "Some of you know me as Elwood Fundy's counselor. It was my privilege to help exorcise the demons that hounded him these many years. Though I, like all of you, will miss him, I am comforted to know that he had resolved the major issues besetting him. He was an unforgettable human being. He gave me as much, if not more, than I gave him. I have come to appreciate conceptual art, for example, thanks to men like Elwood, and Hoskar. We have enjoyed art and music through discussions we have had here at Art's Place, and my life has been enriched. Elwood is now at peace. For those of you not familiar with me, let me just mention that my office is in the Titan Mall, and I'd be more than happy to talk to any friend of Elwood Fundy." He nodded at the box of ashes and gestured with his glass of red wine.

From the assemblage, Hulot Piquete emerged. He stepped to the bar and faced the crowd. "The deceased, here," he began, indicating the shoebox, "was, as you may know, the father of a faculty member at Button Gwinnet Senior High School, and it was in that regard I came to know Mr. Fundy. I must be forthcoming; to know Mr. Fundy was not necessarily to love him. He and I lived on what might be called parallel plains, but I have the sincerest respect for those of you who were better acquainted with him than I. I am present today representing the faculty, students and staff at the high school, showing support to this man's son at his time of loss. I want everyone here to know that like John Donne, every man's death diminishes me. And to Mr. Fundy's son and the rest of you who mourn, may I close with another verse of Donne's: 'Death be not proud, for some have called thee Mighty and dreadful, for thou art not so.' In this life, ere we shuffle off this mortal coil, we are in conflict with the mighty and the dreadful. And from that, Mr. Fundy now enters sweet repose. I join you in saluting him."

"Hear, hear," someone said, as Elwood was toasted once more. Dr. Piquete, seeming to enjoy the attention, bore on. "The burden is incumbent upon we who survive to go forth into what we hope will be ever brighter tomorrows—"

"Oh siddown, ya windy old fart," someone else hollered, and another laughed and cheered. Dr. Piquete blinked, then set his lips and brushed past several men near the bar, pausing for a moment with Richard.

"There's an unruly quality to this gathering, Fundy. I don't approve, just as I did not approve of the influence exerted by your father over your behavior. I came by only to pay my respects. I must say, also, that this seems a most inappropriate venue for a funeral."

"That depends, I suppose," Richard said, moving away. Scowling, Dr. Piquete grabbed his hat and exited Art's Place.

"I know it might sound odd coming from me, Rich," said Luther, sealing a manila envelope and dropping it in the magazine rack next to the sofa in the Fundy living room, "but I have to tell you, I like the old guy's idea of a joke."

"I may not be good for much, Luther," Richard said, placing another envelope in the rack, "but never let it be said I didn't keep my promises. Even though, with my luck, we'll probably get arrested for this." A faint smile flashed across his lips. "And then of course, there'll be absolutely no point in that hearing. I'm done, *nada, niente*. My thinking is to just forget the whole thing. Get away from here and start over someplace else. I can sell Dad's house—I'll sell *Elwood's* house and just go away."

Luther poured a scant handful of ash into another envelope. "You might want to visit Dad You know, talk things over. Maybe he'll talk to you about the culture. He never would with me. Wanted me to adapt and adjust. Guess I did that all right."

"Yeah. It was me who never quite got it right."

"Anyway, I've talked to him twice on the phone. He now admits to a brief affair with your mother, but swears he never knew you might be his. He's remorseful as hell, but says sometimes things that nobody intended, just sort of happen."

"Yeah, I can relate to that." Richard sealed another envelope. "I think that about does it, hey?"

"I'd like to see the looks on folks' faces when they open these."

"Not me. It's sick, Luther, just like the old man."

Luther chuckled. "As the saying goes, Rich, if you're not a little bit sick, you're a bore. Whatever your opinion of Elwood, you have to admit he wasn't a bore."

"Well, I've kept my promise to him, and that's enough. Thing is, how're we going to sneak these envelopes into the mail?"

Luther chuckled again. "I'll take half, you take half, and just drop a few at a time into different out-of-town mail drops. We do it over a couple weeks, and don't have to sneak anything."

Richard grinned. "Yeah. Sure."

"Just leave them here for now. You need to get out of the house, Rich. Let's take a walk."

❖❖❖❖❖

A meander down Mister Lane, a turn left on Snodbody Trail, and the two strolled into a development of houses situated on one-acre lots. Luther skipped stones ahead of them and reminisced about his boyhood as a Native American preacher's kid, who was never schooled in his culture. "We both have some catching up to do, Rich," he said. "That is, if you can conceive of yourself as nearly half Ojibwe."

"In time, Luther. Perhaps in time."

As they continued walking along the flat terrain that their ancestors once roamed as virgin prairie, a tree line emerged at a bend. The maples, absent of leaves now, and pin oaks were bordered by a row of arborvitae.

Luther stopped walking and pulled Richard's sleeve. "Over here," he said, indicating the arborvitae. "Shrubs like this are disappearing all over Carlton County, so it's a treat when you see a good-looking hedge like this." He grinned. "I really miss those out at your place. Anyway, from here we've got one hell of a view of that house and yard."

Michael Fedo is a former folksinger and college professor. His writings have appeared in *The New York Times, Christian Science Monitor, Los Angeles Times,* and numerous literary and commercial magazines. He also has been an essayist on Minnesota Public Radio. He lives in a Minneapolis suburb with his artist-wife, Judy.